WARNING!

ALIENS
are
Invading
the
School!

Look out for Dinah's other hilarious books:

WARNING!
COMPUTERS are Eating my Friend!

WARNING!
VAMPIRES are Living next Door!

WARNING!

ALIENS are Invading the School!

Dinah Capparucci

SCHOLASTIC

Scholastic Children's Books
An imprint of Scholastic Ltd
Euston House, 24 Eversholt Street
London, NW1 1DB, UK
Registered office: Westfield Road, Southam, Warwickshire, CV47 0RA
SCHOLASTIC and associated logos are trademarks and/or registered
trademarks of Scholastic Inc.

First published in the UK as *Aliens Don't Eat Dog Food*, 2008
This edition published 2010

Text copyright © Dinah Capparucci, 2008

The right of Dinah Capparucci to be identified as the author
of this work has been asserted by her.

Cover illustration © Fred Blunt, 2010

ISBN 978 1 407 12422 3

Printed by CPI Bookmarque, Croydon, CR0 4TD
Papers used by Scholastic Children's Books are made from wood grown in
sustainable forests.

1 3 5 7 9 10 8 6 4 2

www.scholastic.co.uk/zone

To my grandmothers Marjorie and
Euvron and Great Auntie Doff,
with love and gratitude.

One

My name is Jordan and my mate's name is Boy Dave (because his dad is Big Dave). To begin with I should say that none of this was our fault. I would have thought that protecting the future of all humanity was a bit more important than they made it out to be. "They" being most of the teachers at school and our parents and also some other people.

All I can say is that it wasn't at all like a film where we would have walked in a line out of the dust to some stirring music. If it had been a film, obviously two of us would have died while we were protecting the future of all humanity and that would have been a fat, lazy one, who showed he was quite brave in the end, and also a quite good-looking one who was bad and then became good just long enough to die a hero, although we couldn't exactly have done it like that because there were only three of us.

Somewhere out there in the universe there may be a few aliens who were a bit impressed by our attempts and this might help the future of all humanity in the long run. All I can say is that there were some

1

members of humanity who didn't deserve to be saved and I hope the aliens have made a note of who they were.

Most of it was Ryan's idea. In the film he would be the weird genius who no one listens to at first and then everyone has to beg him to help them at the last minute. Boy Dave and I don't bother with the middle bit and just listen to him first time, which in this case might have been part of the problem.

We were sitting in a boat we'd borrowed from outside the Black Horse pub. It was the last weekend of the summer holidays and it hadn't rained for about four days. We'd done most of the things we'd planned to do, but this morning was the day for our trip on the stream. You have to get up early for this or they notice one of the boats has gone, but, being a pub, the Black Horse doesn't open until eleven, so as long as you get the boat back by nine thirty it's normally OK. Boy Dave and I are banned from going near the Black Horse and this was something to do with a plastic tree-climbing frame, which I can't really remember.

Ryan doesn't like rowing, so Boy Dave and I had the oars. That morning it was misty with lots of dragonflies whirling over the surface of the water. The swans were there too, but they're incredibly bad-tempered and don't like it if you make eye contact.

Ryan was in the middle of dissecting a dragonfly

when he suddenly looked serious.

"I've been meaning to mention some research I've been doing," he said, pushing his glasses up his nose. "It has to do with extraterrestrial beings and is probably quite important."

Boy Dave and I looked at each other. We like Ryan but sometimes he can be a bit boring.

"It's quite obvious that aliens exist," he said. "Quite a lot of people have been abducted by them, especially in America. I think they mostly abduct Americans because the FBI try to hide all the attempts the aliens have made to contact planet earth."

Boy Dave said, "All that alien stuff is boring."

But when Ryan gets on to one of his obsessions it's impossible to stop him.

"That's exactly why it's important that people like me take an interest and try to understand the messages," he said. "Here on earth we have examples of metal which can't have been mined or made. There are whole spaceships which definitely haven't come from this planet, and bodies of aliens hidden away in basements to try and pretend they don't exist."

"That's just made up." Boy Dave pushed away an overhanging branch with his oar. "Everyone knows it's people with tinfoil hats who live in trailers and just want to get on TV."

Ryan shook his head. "I've been on the Internet and there's accounts of serious people who have actually seen them. Like ex-FBI agents who think we should know the truth."

"How do they know they're not just plastic models?" demanded Boy Dave. "You never see live aliens, just dead ones that all look the same."

Ryan rattled his jar crossly. Inside was a tatty-looking moth and another dragonfly who was probably absolutely terrified after what had just happened to his friend. "Small point." (Ryan always says this.) "If they go to all that trouble pretending aliens don't exist, then they're not really going to make a plastic one and show it to someone and pretend it's real are they?"

It was just after nine o' clock. Andy, the landlord of the Black Horse, comes out for his first fag at quarter to ten to wait for the draymen, so we had to be getting back. Boy Dave and I paddled the boat round in a circle. The mist was lifting; it was going to be another sunny day.

Suddenly Ryan started pointing at the air.

"If we don't do something to show the aliens that someone actually takes them seriously, they're going to come down one day, with a big alien army, and take over the planet. The future of all humanity depends on making positive contact. Negative contact will end in the complete annihilation of the human race."

Talking of complete annihilation, we managed to

get the boat back under the tarpaulin just as Andy came out wearing a pair of stripy pyjama bottoms. As we sneaked round the other side of the Black Horse and across the road Ryan said in a sinister voice, "The preparations are in hand."

Two

When I got in, Dad and Auntie Dulcie were sitting waiting for breakfast. It being a Saturday we were meant to be having a full English but, by the smoke coming from the kitchen, it wasn't going very well. Dad was in a bad mood.

"All this rubbish about sick pay." He was reading a copy of *The Sun*. "When I was young, if you didn't work you didn't get paid."

My dad and Big Dave have a building company called Rise Building Contractors. Boy Dave told me they're a man down and that's why they have to work Saturdays at the moment. One of their blokes fell off the ladder when he was carrying a hod of bricks and a brick landed on Mrs White's Pekinese dog and it had to go to the vet's and have something done to its tail. She made our dads pay for it.

I should say at this point, because it's important for later, that Mrs White's dog is called Confucius. It looks like a cute Disney character but is totally vicious. It glides along the pavement, making a hideous yapping noise and you can't see its legs moving, so it's like being attacked by a small, psychotic, furry hovercraft.

The smoke alarm went off in the kitchen and Mum yelled, "Dominic! Push the red button."

Dad carried on reading his paper.

Mum appeared in the doorway. Her face was the colour of the red button. "Now!"

Dad put down his paper grumpily and went into the kitchen. The noise stopped. Auntie Dulcie, who was sitting at the table sewing up a pair of jeans, said, "I remember the days when people managed to switch things on and off without red buttons."

"Red buttons aren't just for switching things on and off," I told her. "There's one for complete global destruction and also one on the Sky remote."

Dulcie carried on sewing. "Well, we managed two world wars without one, and as for *Sky*," (she pulled a snobby face) "I'm sure when they tell those of us at home to push our red buttons, that it's only a small handful of very piteous and troubled individuals who actually do it."

I should say at this point that although we call her "Auntie Dulcie" I don't think anyone really knows who she is or where she came from. Dad once said that she was my mum's aunt, but seeing as he hates all our relatives and, so far, to get out of seeing them we have:

* been off on holiday
* all been very ill
* had a flood
* said that the car, the van and the work truck have all been broken on the same day

I'm sure he hasn't spoken to any of them long enough to know. I think it's more likely that Auntie Dulcie is some sort of elderly impostor. She probably infiltrated loads of other families before she came to us, but was always unmasked when the weird relatives who only come round at Christmas poked their noses in and started asking awkward questions as they ate mince pies. This hasn't been a problem at ours, because Dulcie has got really good at pretending to be deaf and if any relatives do manage to slip through the net they normally go home early because Dad is a bit too rude. (Actually there was someone called Derrick who mainly talked about food and germs, who Dad was *really* rude to, and he stayed for quite a long time, but that's another story.)

Point being, Dulcie infiltrated us when I was quite little, and, so far, no one's ever been able to prove she isn't who she says she is. She's supposed to have been a respectable English teacher but you only have to hear some of the ridiculous words she comes out with to get suspicious. Anyway, she's like a proper member of the family now and I really like her, which is the main thing.

Mum appeared with two plates of burnt sausages, bacon, mushrooms and a sort of yellow splodge, which was probably an egg. She glared at me. "I've had Andy on the phone. What were you doing hanging round the Black Horse this morning?"

I stared. Obviously the whole village is involved in the black arts and different people become hares or crows or black cats to spy on us. And these are mostly members of the Women's Institute.

"We went for a walk by the stream," I said. "In case you hadn't noticed we're not actually banned from going for walks by the stream."

"Don't be cheeky!' She banged down my plate and the egg thing slid off the side. Dad shuffled in behind her. He pretends that he only has a full English breakfast once a week on Saturdays, but he and Big Dave go to the cafe at eleven o'clock every morning and have one there.

"You'd better not have been messing about on those boats again," he told me.

Luckily Joanna made her entrance then.

Joanna's my sister. She's fifteen, three years older than me, and lives in a parallel universe. This is like a continuous episode of *Friends*, *One Tree Hill*, *Hollyoaks*, and other programmes that are mainly on E4. She was wearing pink pyjamas with "cute" written on the T-shirt. It should have said "vile".

"I heard, like, a screeching noise?" (Joanna turns everything into a question.) "And it, like, woke me?"

"Yeah," I told her, "there was, *like*, two big rats and one ate the other and it howled in agony and its entrails—"

"Jordan!" said Mum. "Eat your food."

"You'll be pleased to know," Dulcie held up her sewing, "that I've mended your trousers."

It's quite unusual for Joanna to be lost for words.

"Thank you, Dulcie," said Mum quickly, "it was very thoughtful of you."

Joanna went, "Uhh?"

I should say at this point that Joanna's ripped jeans were her best ones and they are meant to be ripped. I also think Dulcie actually knew that.

Joanna took an apple from the fruit bowl and made a massive drama about it, so that Mum said, "That all you're having?"

Joanna flicked her hair about. "Some of us like to eat healthily."

"She's got a packet of biscuits under her bed," I said (I'd been storing this one up to use against her for ages). "Well – she did have."

Joanna gave me a death stare.

"Oh," said Dulcie, "like Sartre's Ivitch. She kept a pot of jam under hers. If I remember rightly, she stuck a knife in her hand as well."

"I don't want to be rude, Auntie," said Joanna sweetly, "but I think you went senile in the night?"

Mum said, "So anyway, what are the plans for today?"

I kept quiet. As soon as you start telling grown-ups things they start interfering.

"Hel-looo," said Joanna. "Like, the concert to welcome all the new parents to the school?"

"Oh, we haven't forgotten, darling," said Mum hastily, "but that's not until next Saturday."

"For you." Joanna looked hard done by. "I'm in rehearsals all day."

"You should join a choir, Jordan," said Mum, obviously liking the "all day" bit. "It would do you good to take up a hobby."

Dulcie said, "I always think collecting birds' eggs is a good hobby for a boy."

"Yes," said Joanna spitefully, "or you could take up trainspotting."

"Oh no, dear," Dulcie put on her remembering face, "not after poor Roddy. He was a trainspotter. He was engaged to my chum Kitty. I *think*. . ." she crinkled her eyes, "they'd even arranged the wedding. Yes they had, because I was supposed to wear some ghastly pink dress made from a net curtain. They found

Roddy's notebook by the side of the train track. It was all very unfortunate."

Joanna put her hand on her chest. "That is *so* tragic."

"Not really, dear," said Dulcie. "He was the most boring person. And, of course, there were lots of dishy GIs around at the time. Yes," she nodded to herself, "Kitty went on to have quite a good war after that."

It was round about now that we heard the click-clunk of the post dropping through the door.

Three

Dad always tries to get other people to read letters because reading takes him ages and he finds it boring. He came back from the hall with an envelope and said that pointless thing grown-ups always say: "Don't know who this one's from." He handed it to Mum.

"I'm still eating, give it to Dulcie."

"Oh," Dulcie peered at the envelope wisely, "it's from the school." (I started to feel a bit uncomfortable; letters from school are normally very one-sided.) "It says something about – I should really have my reading glasses – er . . . sombrero, no, that's a Mexican hat. Stagnant, possibly. Strangled? Oh, here we are, reliquary – that's a container for holy relics. Telegram . . . I see, I think they're referring to a document about stag beetles."

"Dulcie darling," sighed Mum, "you're guessing. You'd better give it to me. Let me see. It says that the school has agreed to take part in a . . . oh," for some reason she gave me a sudden nervous look, ". . .reality television show this term, about the students. We

13

have to sign a consent form to say our children can take part."

Dad frowned. "I don't agree with all that rubbish. Write back and say our two can't be in it."

Joanna, who had been sitting with her eyes getting wider and wider like an excited, and yet strangely dying fish, suddenly went, "Oh . . . my . . . God! I'm going to be on television."

And Mum, who had been carrying on reading, said worriedly to Dad, "I don't know, Dom. The school's going to be given some money for it. You know how desperate they are for funding. Anyway, it sounds quite good. It's got that Dr Agnetha – you know – the Mega Psyche. She's that one who goes into schools and sorts out problem classes."

"That is just so what I need," said Joanna. "Someone I can really talk to about my problems."

"I think it's more if the children are out of control," said Mum. "I saw one where there was this really nasty gang of mouthy young girls and Dr Agnetha turned them into absolute angels. I think, by the end, they were all sewing dollies for Rumanian orphans."

"That's great," said Joanna enthusiastically. "Auntie Dulcie can spend Sunday teaching me to sew."

By now Dad had his mouth really full of bacon and eggs and couldn't talk, so he had to make do with pulling a disapproving face, but even when he'd

14

finished he didn't say anything. The truth is he tries to avoid telling Joanna she can't do something, because it always turns into a massive great drama that lasts for weeks.

As for me, I thought it would be the same as all the school processions and plays and stuff: when Joanna has a massive part and me and Boy Dave aren't even allowed to audition. By Monday I'd forgotten all about it.

The first day back at school is always terrible. It's like the moment when the judge says, "TAKE HIM DOWN," and the prisoner looks really shocked and shouts, "I'M INNOCENT, I TELL YOU," and they drag him away through a little dark door. Last year was our first time in this school. Before that me, Ryan and Boy Dave all went to this tiny little one, where there were only about ten in each class, so Hatton Down seemed huge, but once we got used to it, it kind of shrank – so instead of really getting lost on the way to lessons you had to start pretending.

Mum gave me a new school uniform and a pencil case, and said in a really nasty voice, "This year had better be an improvement on the last one."

My old uniform was just starting to feel comfy, whereas this new one was only ever going to fit if I became a giant, and the pencil case was practically empty because on mine and Boy Dave's equipment lists someone had written, *No sharp edges or compasses*, then, underneath, *rubbers only if on the end of pencils*. I did try and explain that everyone knows rubbers on the end of pencils are rubbish and just smudge everything around a bit, but Mum was trying to do cornrow plaits in Joanna's hair and was in the sort of bad mood that makes her go deaf.

That Monday, the first people we saw were Connor Keefe and Cal Mockford. They'd managed to persuade their mums to buy them huge hooded puffas like some of the older kids, and were now on the steps to the main entrance trying to look hard. I think Connor found it pretty tough last year: going from being one of the biggest to one of the smallest; and he was probably really glad there was going to be a new supply of smaller people to bully this year.

"Connor mate," said Boy Dave as we pushed past them, "you accidentally wore your bed to school."

Connor looked mean. "Get lost."

"Yeah," said Cal, "before he makes you."

"You should try rolling down the steps in that," I told him. "You're so puffy you're probably invincible."

But the good feeling we got from annoying Connor and Cal wore off pretty quickly.

It was as if during the summer holidays they'd tried to remove all traces of us kids from the school. Everything smelled lemony and was spookily clean, and the floor of the main corridor was really shiny and squeaked when you walked on it. On the walls were lots of big arrows made out of coloured paper with things like *Yr7 Maths* and *Yr7 English* written on them. I suppose they got a bit fed up of everyone getting lost last year. Anyway, someone had already moved them all about, so year seven were going to be lucky if they even made it to assembly.

Boy Dave and me walked slowly past the lines of lockers.

"It's like those horses," I said eventually. "They get them on the end of ropes and shout at them and hit them with sticks, and the horse tries to get away and goes ne-e-e-eigh and kicks. . ."

Boy Dave nodded gloomily. "And then they break its spirit."

We walked on in silence for a bit.

Boy Dave said, "Or that thing where they plug you into the mains and burn out your brain."

"And that torture where they drip water on your head until you go mad."

I think we'd decided to try and cheer ourselves up with a couple of bars of chocolate and had automatically made our way to the vending machine. But when we got there, there was a big bit of white paper stuck inside the glass. It said, *As part of this term's healthy eating policy, only fruit and vegetables are allowed on school premises.*

We stared in horror at the empty metal shelves.

"We'll starve," said Boy Dave in a hollow voice.

If there's an opposite to the expression "the icing on the cake", then this was it.

"We can bunk out to the shop at break," I said at last.

"That's hours away." Boy Dave gave me a pitying look. "Still, I suppose at least all the bad things have happened now."

Which belonged to the group of things you should never ever say, like, "It's stayed nice and sunny so far" and "Nothing can possibly go wrong now".

Four

We found Ryan somewhere between the vending machine and the school theatre where we go for assembly. He was staring up at a silver ball, which was fixed to the ceiling like a sort of lampshade. To my mind it looked a bit like a bowling ball, with a black dot on the side.

"They're everywhere." Ryan frowned. "I've been trying to work out how to get one down and have a look at it." (By which he meant dismantle.) "And look at these," he pushed open the classroom door behind him, "little dangly things."

Inside the classroom was another silver ball and about five small black lumps hanging by thin wires from the ceiling.

"Forget it," said Boy Dave carelessly. "It's probably just new decorations. Right now, we've got a serious problem with the supplies to sort out."

We told Ryan about the vending machine, but you could see the ceiling things were still bugging him. All the way to assembly he kept looking around for more.

"Look," I said kindly, "once we've sorted out the

19

sweets we'll have a go at getting one down for you to ... er ... look at, OK?

Our school theatre, which they use as the assembly hall, isn't a proper theatre at all. It's more like a football pitch, with rows of seats going up all around and the standing/stage bit as a square at the bottom. As usual we headed for the top row, while the headmistress made a big point of standing in the middle looking up sternly until everyone stopped talking. Then she said, "Right, this term forms will be year eleven, Mr Fern, year ten, Miss Robertson, year nine, Mr Jefferson" (a small whisper went round the room and we stared pityingly over at the year nines, who hung their heads miserably) "year eight, Miss Fairjoy." (Boy Dave nudged me – better than Jefferson, but not so good as Miss Robertson, who looks a bit like Beyonce) "And year seven – welcome to Hatton Down – your form tutor will be Mrs Clark."

Those members of year seven who weren't still lost, stared down with big eyes. They all looked really small and way too neat. It was strange to think that last year that was us. Still, they'd got a seriously senile form tutor, so it was a good start.

"There's someone I'd like you all to meet," the head continued. "This is Dr Barns." Dr Barns was shaped like a triangle and had massive white teeth like an upside-down igloo.

"Please," she beamed round, "you guys call me Agnetha."

They quite often have boring people visiting in assembly. Like the man with a load of bees in a sort of glass window. He went on and on about "delicious honey" and kept pointing at the bees, saying, "Now you see this one here? See how he dances to show all the other bees where to go to gather the nectar to make *delicious honey*." Obviously he was standing right down on the stage, so we could only just about see the glass thing and definitely couldn't see bees doing any dancing.

Not being particularly interested in delicious honey, we don't normally listen to guest speakers in assembly, but this time it seemed important to see The Agnetha from all angles in case she was actually a human pyramid, and I kept imagining a medium-sized tribe of Eskimos trying to escape through her teeth.

"There will be a small television crew with me," she was saying. She had a weird foreign-sounding accent. "And you will also be monitored by CCTV cameras. Now," (she gave everyone a "you won't be silly, will you?" look) "it's nothing to worry about. Most kids get really used to it. We'll be monitoring your progress and there will be lots of opportunities to win rewards for changing negative behaviour to positive behaviour. Let me remind you of a cute little saying."

She looked like she was really pleased with this one. "When we feel the urge to do something that we know is wrong, what do you think we say?" She wagged a finger in the air. "That's right. We just say *'No to Mr Negative!'* What do we say?"

There was complete silence.

"That's right," she pretended we'd all shouted at once, *"No to Mr Negative!"*

For some reason I remembered what Ryan had said about negative contact resulting in the complete annihilation of the human race.

That first lesson, Poppy Lockhart and Emma Chichester came and plonked themselves right beside us. Poppy has a big round face like a moon (everything about Poppy is round), and Emma is like a sort of fur-free white mouse with a pink nose. I should say at this point that girls seem to really like Boy Dave. My mum says it's because he's "pretty", which is a bit of an insult; I'd say it's because he looks a bit like David Beckham. Also he always talks like he's got a sore throat, which is most likely from shouting so much. Girls seem to like that as well – the sore throat, I mean, not the shouting. Poppy Lockhart once said to him, "Do you know you've got a really nice husky voice?" And Boy Dave said, "You've got a voice like my dad's farts," which didn't go down very well, but Poppy Lockhart has goldfish genes and forgets things too easily.

Now Poppy was leaning over Boy Dave's desk.

"Have you done your summer project?"

"What?" Boy Dave glared at her.

"You know, the one about designing all the measurements of a house?"

Me and Boy Dave looked at each other. We couldn't remember anything about any measurements of a house. We looked over at Ryan, who said, "I think I made a start on it, but then I had an idea for the alien project. Practically speaking, there's no real reason to do measurements for something which you're never going to build."

Under the circumstances this wasn't strictly true. Given that, any minute now, a maniac was going to walk through the door and *want* them, there was probably quite a good reason to have designed all the measurements for something we were never going to build.

Jefferson shouldn't actually be a teacher. Teachers are mostly slightly smelly and boring with terrible clothes, and a bad sense of humour. Jefferson is an ex-army (and I'm going to say this in such a way so as not to be cruel) *lunatic*, with absolutely *no* sense of humour. His voice is so loud it can shatter eardrums five football pitches away (which, by the way, is the same distance that a shark can smell the blood of its prey).

"You can copy mine," said Poppy to Boy Dave.

"No thank you, Poopy," said Boy Dave, "I'll just do it myself really quickly." He started drawing a sort of house shape, with measurements written down the sides like our dads do on their drawings. "Hmm. Right. Roof: ten by four mil, wall: three by six. Door, that's got to be smaller than the walls; let's say one by point five."

It was a bit like listening to Dulcie trying to read a letter without her glasses.

At that moment Jefferson made his entrance.

Five

Jefferson marched over to the desk and knocked on it loudly.

"Attention," he said.

We all got tiredly to our feet.

"Good morning, sir."

"Inspection," he said. "Battle dress. Full kit."

Jefferson treats everything like the army and it's best just to go along with it. Everyone started to get all the things out of their pencil cases and lay them out in rows.

"Set squares times two, protractor, pencil sharpener," Jefferson marched up and down between the desks, "compass, divider, rubber, ruler, pencil, pen." (Like when we're grown-up we're all going to go: I don't feel like using my computer today. I think I'll do the whole design using the antique things that I keep in my pencil case.)

When he got to us Jefferson stopped.

"We're ... er ... not allowed sharp edges," I explained.

"Or rubbers," added Boy Dave.

"And why is you not allowed sharp edges?" asked Jefferson in an enquiring sort of voice.

We blinked nervously. Jefferson normally prefers to answer his own questions. "Perhaps you is not allowed sharp edges," he suggested, "because you do PLAY DARTS WITH YOUR COMPASSES.

"AND YOU DO MAKE 'ORRIBLE MARKS ON THE TABLES.

"YOU IS NOT ALLOWED SHARP EDGES BECAUSE YOU IS A LIABILITY WITH SHARP EDGES.

"YOU IS NOT ALLOWED RUBBERS BECAUSE YOU DO PING THEM.

"AND AS A RESULT OF THIS PINGING AND THIS DARTING AND THIS 'ORRIBLE MARKING – YOU DOES NOT 'AVE THE PROPER KIT FOR THIS LESSON."

He did that creepy thing of suddenly going quiet again – like a racing car that conks out and starts to hiss under the bonnet.

"And boys what do not 'ave the proper kit for my lessonsss will suffer the consequencesssah."

"Yes, sir," we mumbled feebly.

I did try to stop Boy Dave from handing in his "summer project", but it's a bit difficult to whisper really quickly to someone who's on his way up to the teacher's desk that they've just designed an insect-sized cathedral.

*

If you see someone hopping at Hatton Down Community School, it probably has something to do with Jefferson. To cut a long story short, me, Boy Dave and Ryan were to stay behind after class and hop up and down the corridor ten times. It was lap three, and we were starting to get a bit red and out of breath, when the headmistress and The Agnetha appeared.

The head of our school is like a posh woman from a war film; she wears suits that are made of green and brown carpets and her tights are really baggy. She stays in her office most of the time drinking little glasses of water. (This is because she is nocturnal and prefers to perform her duties under cover of darkness.) When she and The Agnetha saw us all hopping towards them they stopped and looked a bit surprised. Then the head tried to pretend we weren't real and carried on walking.

"And these classrooms are equipped with projectors and touch-sensitive display thingies," she said grandly.

The Agnetha looked confused. "Those boys are hopping up and down."

"Yes indeed," said the head. "We're very environmentally friendly here, and only use low-wattage bulbs."

"But they are hopping," said The Agnetha, "up and down."

Jefferson, who had been standing at the other end

of the corridor counting laps said, "They is hopping to remind them to do their school projects and keep their kit up straight, ma'am."

"You mean to say this is some sort of a punishment?" The Agnetha turned accusingly to the head. "But this is draconian."

The head coughed. "I think that might be enough for today, Mr Jefferson."

"No, ma'am," said Jefferson. "They 'as done three and they 'as seven to go."

"Seven!" said The Agnetha. "You will damage their spines."

"Oh, I don't know," said the head in a jolly voice, "I used to thoroughly enjoy a game of hopscotch when I was a gal."

"Damage, ma'am?" said Jefferson. "There are some men in this great country of ours what think nothing of running up and down hills with refrigerators on their backs."

"Quite, Mr Jefferson," said the head hastily. "But I expect they are members of the SAS."

While they'd been having this conversation, me, Boy Dave and Ryan had kind of ground to a halt. Jefferson must have noticed, because he suddenly yelled, "FOUR!"

"No," said The Agnetha. "Do not hop any more."

"FOUR!" shouted Jefferson again.

"NO!" shouted The Agnetha even louder.

"Mr Jefferson," said the head sternly, "commendable though your dedication to discipline is, I think perhaps you may be being slightly overzealous on this occasion. Run along now, boys," she said heartily.

As we thankfully gathered up our bags and started off down the corridor we heard Jefferson saying something about wishy-washy socialists and how it was their fault decent people were scared to walk the streets. And The Agnetha said something about not going back to Victorian times and kids needing love and understanding.

As we walked across the playground Boy Dave said, "I wasn't too keen on this reality TV stuff at first, but that Agnetha doesn't seem that bad."

"It would be quite good if she goes round trying to give us love and understanding all the time," I agreed. "We could get away with loads."

Six

It was supposed to be English with Miss Fairjoy after break, but when we got into class there was no one there. After about five minutes we started to wonder if they'd forgotten about us. A few rubbers, or, in our case, pencils, started flying about and (as you do) someone put a cup of water on the door. After a bit longer we started to play islands and sharks, which is where everyone has to jump on the desks (islands), and the sharks have to get you off. Some of the girls started being really boring and said they were going to get a teacher, but, just as they were gathering up all their millions of items into their pencil cases, the classroom door slowly opened.

By rights, whoever it was on the other side should have been drenched when the cup of water fell on them, but they had pressed themselves right up against the other side of the door, out of the way.

"Hi there," The Agnetha appeared suddenly and stepped over the puddle, "sorry I've been so long, I was collecting these little guys."

She plonked a large brown sack on the desk, like

the one the farmer uses to carry his ferrets. I started to wonder if The Agnetha had maybe brought some ferrets in as classroom pets. We used to have classroom pets in little school, but me and Boy Dave never got to look after them in the holidays. Ryan was once allowed to take home the tetra fish, but I'm afraid that didn't go very well.

"Now," said The Agnetha, "who would like to go first?"

Boy Dave really likes animals, so he quickly put his hand up.

"Great." She beamed at him. "Come on up and choose one."

Boy Dave went up to the desk and stuck his head in the sack.

"It should be the one that best describes you," said The Agnetha.

Boy Dave took his head back out of the sack and stared at her as if she had gone mad.

"Like, for instance, if I thought I was the sort of person who remembered things," she reached in and pulled out a toy elephant, "I might choose this little guy. Or if I thought I was a prickly, difficult to know, sort of person, I might choose her." She took out a toy hedgehog with a hat and apron.

By this time Boy Dave had started to go red and look back at his seat.

"How about this little hippo?" coaxed The Agnetha.

Some people started to giggle and Boy Dave decided enough was enough. "None of them." He stomped back to his desk.

There was a sudden big noise as the girls all went, "I'll do it. I'll do it."

"This one, because he's a turtle who likes swimming and I really like swimming."

"I'm the lion, because I can be really fierce."

"I'm the lizard because. . ." (*slightly* worrying) "I can change colours to wherever I am."

Even Connor decided to be a giraffe who likes eating leaves, but, to be fair to him, I don't think he really got the point.

Once everyone was back at their desks with their cuddly-toy selves, The Agnetha looked over at me, Boy Dave and Ryan.

"Now, which one of you is most like this little penguin? And this little bear here – or perhaps this cute little monkey? Something tells me," she twinkled, "that we might need three little monkeys."

We slithered as far down in our seats as we could go. It wasn't the cuddly toys as such. When we were small, me and Boy Dave had Panda and Blue Dog, and Ryan had a revolving whisk, but nowadays Panda and Blue Dog both have shelves and are more like decorations, and I think Ryan's whisk went back to the kitchen. In any event cuddly toys are seriously private things and should never ever be seen in public. To make matters worse some people started trying to choose for us and it all got pretty insulting actually.

The Agnetha came over and put the penguin, the koala and the monkey in front of us.

"Now," she said to the whole class, "I'm going to ask you all to do something that might sound a little strange. I'd like you – right now – to pick up your little animal selves and give them a great big hug!"

Some of the other boys said, "Ahhhh," really loudly and after the hugs they looked at each other and started laughing and punching the bears, but they weren't fooling anyone. The girls weren't even pretending not to like it.

I sat and stared gloomily at my penguin. Up until then I'd had no idea that this sort of stuff existed. In our village there are some people who the vicar calls emissaries of the devil, and my dad says this is because they go round hugging trees. I started to wonder if The Agnetha was this kind of person – but like an extreme, converting-everyone sort, with really strongly held beliefs.

I was woken up from these thoughts by Ryan tapping my arm. He was staring really fixedly up at one of the silver balls. I sighed; this wasn't really the time to start worrying about the ceiling things. But Ryan tapped me again, really urgently. Finally I looked up too.

It was the first time I'd really looked at one of the

silver balls. It was fixed to a round bit on the ceiling by two flat plastic strips, which went on either side of the silver ball. It was similar to how the front forks on a bike fix on to the wheel. Suddenly, all on its own, the plastic circle twisted silently and creepily from one side to the other. A few seconds later, the silver ball rolled all the way round. For a second I thought Ryan had learned to move things with his mind but then he scribbled a single word in tiny writing on his desk: *camera*.

The Agnetha said loudly, "That was great! We come to learn that a little self-love goes a long way. But how about the person next to you? It's great to love ourselves, but what about showing other people we value them? And feeling valued by other people? I think this time we all need to stand up."

Like zombies our class all got to their feet. Above our heads, the sliver ball stared from one person to another interestedly, from its round black eye.

"Now," said The Agnetha, "I want you to turn to the person next to you. That's right," she said joyfully, "turn around. Now guess what? You're going to give them a great big hug too!"

I don't think we ever thought there would be a day when we looked forward to games with Jefferson, but this was it. As the rest of our class were all, rather embarrassedly, doing the great big hugs, there was a distant rumbling outside and the first flash of white lightning lit up the hills and fields.

Seven

By the time we headed out to the top field the rain was hammering down and the sky was dark as night. Boy Dave didn't seem to have even noticed. He still hadn't recovered his pride from being the first to almost choose a cuddly toy.

"No way,' he said for the millionth time. "No way am I having anything else to do with that stupid reality TV rubbish."

"I'm really glad we didn't do it," I said. "It would be all on the film by now."

"She called us monkeys!" said Boy Dave, fuming. "Wait till my dad hears about this."

"Talking of monkeys," said Ryan, "they must have been filming us like some sort of wildlife programme, before The Agnetha even came in. How else could she have known about the water on the door? Those cameras can rotate three hundred and sixty degrees and turn on the axis of the fitting, which means they can see every single thing that happens in our class. And hear. I'll bet you anything those black, dangly wires are microphones."

I frowned. "Why, though? It's not like anything interesting ever happens in class."

"Well, anyway," said Boy Dave, "I'm going to say we don't want to be in it any more."

"They won't take much notice of that," said Ryan knowingly. "Our parents have signed that bit of paper."

We had reached the pathetic little wooden shelter at the top of the field where the rest of our class were huddling in shorts and T-shirts and Jefferson was walking slowly up and down with his hands behind his back.

"You 'as 'ad your 'olidays," he told us, "and you is now refreshed." (He said this as if he, too, was suddenly feeling refreshed.) "But in your 'olidays you 'as allowed yourselves to get SLACK. You 'as allowed yourselves to get FAT." (He yelled this in Steven Longacre's face.) "You 'as allowed yourselves to get LAZY." (Boy Dave's face.) "But, as providence would 'ave it, we 'as a remedy for this SLACKNESS, this FATNESS and this LAZINESS, do we not?"

Through the rain you could just make out the white markers pinned to trees in the woods across the stream. Jefferson had arranged a cross-country run.

"Please, sir," said Poppy Lockhart nervously, "I don't think you're meant to go out in thunderstorms."

Jefferson looked surprised and held his hand out of

the shelter, where it almost got splattered to jelly. "Merely a drop of light summer rain," he said in his "refreshed" voice. "What never 'urt no one."

Then he made us all put on yellow reflector strips, so we didn't get run over in the monsoon.

Once we were across the bridge and into the woods Boy Dave, Ryan and me hid behind a bush until the others had gone past. Not including the one we had just crossed, the quickest way back to school was another bridge about a mile away. Jefferson waits in the shelter watching the first bridge, which means you have to somehow get to the second bridge and run back in time for lunch. If you don't, you miss lunch. It's almost foolproof from Jefferson's point of view.

What me, Boy Dave and Ryan normally do is go a little way along and slide back down the bank. Then we sort of swim/wade back across. After that it's easy enough to crawl along the edge of the bank until we're out of sight. Obviously at some point we have to jog back towards the school from the other direction but apart from that we have almost an hour of slightly wet free time. The only problem we had today was how to sneak back in and get our dinner money. Ryan reckoned that the vending machine being out of action had created a serious gap in the market.

"If we buy a chocolate bar for forty-five pence," he had explained a little bit earlier, "we could sell it at school for sixty pence. So for every twenty we sold. . ." (He looked grandly up at the sky as if working out some big scientific problem.) ". . .we would make a pound each."

"Well, we'll sell them for seventy pence each, then," said Boy Dave, "and then we'll make. . ." he too looked up at the sky, "more than that."

Unfortunately our dinner money was in the lockers in the main corridor.

"If we get caught we'll just say we finished the race early," said Boy Dave.

Ryan looked at his watch. "Hmm, that would mean we'd run two miles in ten minutes."

We were crouched down at the edge of the playground, just past the end of the upper field. It was the first time we'd ever tried to sneak *in* to school.

"It's not far to the side door," said Boy Dave, "and in this rain, there's a good chance they won't see us."

"I'd never make it." Ryan tried to polish his glasses on his completely drenched T-shirt. "I can't see a thing. It might be best if just one of us goes."

"That's you," Boy Dave said to me. "You're the fastest. They might even believe you'd finished the race really quickly."

"OK, but what if someone asks what I'm doing at the lockers?"

"Say you were getting your medicine for your illness."

They both punched me to wish me luck and then, with a last look around, I scrambled up the bank and bolted for the side door.

Back inside everything was really hushed except for the sounds of lessons going on in the distance. It's one of those things about being out in the rain that you never realize how wet you are until you get indoors. A huge puddle dripped down round my feet, and my trainers made a loud sort of squelch/squeak on the floor. Still, all I had to do was get our money and get out again.

I'd managed to sneak down the hall and past the staffroom, and was almost at the main corridor when I realized there was one thing we hadn't counted on: I was going to have to make it right past the headmistress's office. Worst of all, the door was slightly open and there were voices coming from inside.

"What we really need for the programme," I recognized The Agnetha's foreign-sounding accent, "is a focus; something I can get my teeth into."

I heard the headmistress say, "How do you mean get your teeth into, Dr Barns?"

"Well," said The Agnetha, "as you know I'm a

39

psychologist who specializes in dealing with disruptive and difficult behaviour. I was wondering if there were any particular kids who have been causing the school problems?"

"Hmm," said the headmistress. "Are you sure you won't have a sherry, Dr Barns?"

I was quite interested, but there wasn't time to stay and listen. Nervously I sploshed on past.

I got Ryan's and Boy Dave's money out with no major setbacks and was just getting mine when I heard footsteps coming from the small corridor. Quickly I shut my locker and was about to make a bolt for it when the head's voice said loudly, "Just a moment, young man!"

Eight

The head and The Agnetha advanced towards me.

"Dear me," said The Agnetha, "this boy is wet through."

The head gave me a stern look. "Why aren't you out there with the rest of your class?"

"I . . . er . . . well," I said casually, "I'm just a very fast runner. I finished the run before all the others, so I quickly came in here to get my medicine for my. . ." I searched my mind for a good-sounding illness and came up with one of Dulcie's, "touch of angina."

"The children had to go running in this?" said The Agnetha, pointing to the torrential downpour outside. "And when this poor boy suffers from a heart complaint?"

The head glared at me.

"Really," continued The Agnetha, "this is terrible. Those poor kids. You know, it's very important that we treat our children the way we, ourselves, would like to be treated." She turned to me. "I remember you from this morning. What's your name?"

I started to wish I'd never even tried to get the

41

money for the stupid sweets; the last thing I wanted was The Agnetha remembering me.

"Erm, Jordan," I mumbled, "Jordan Smith."

"So you're Jordan." She gave me a sudden interested look. "Hmm. Well, you must go and have a warm shower and the rest of the children must be brought in at once."

"That might be a bit difficult," I told her. "They're all out running in the woo—"

"THANK you, Jordan," said the headmistress loudly.

By the time I got back to Boy Dave and Ryan they'd almost given up on me.

"It's like the head has to go along with everything she says," I told them on the way to the shop. "The Agnetha rushed out to have a go at Jefferson and there was nothing she could do about it."

Ryan, who was practically blind from the rain on his glasses, was feebly holding his hands out in front of him, trying to feel his way along the street. "The school's getting paid to do the show. They'll do anything for money."

"If I had lots of money," said Boy Dave, "I'd make some big changes round here, believe me." He turned back to Ryan. "You'd better hold on to my shoulder, or we'll never get there."

"By the way," I told Ryan casually, "I found this 'cute little guy' in your locker." I reached into my pocket and pulled out the koala bear.

"Oh," said Ryan, peering through rain-drenched glasses. "Him."

Boy Dave goggled. "You kept your toy?"

"I've got quite a few of them," Ryan told him. "When we had to put them all away in the sack, I grabbed a couple of handfuls and popped them in my bag. I got the hedgehog," he added proudly.

I should say at this point that, unless you count dismembering them to get out the growly/talkie/ mechanical bits, Ryan has never understood the concept of toys. I would have liked to think that he secretly wanted a little companion to hold and be his silent friend, and that he had just been too embarrassed to admit it – except that Ryan never gets embarrassed. I'm afraid to say I began to fear for the little guys' safety, especially, probably, the hedgehog.

When I got home that evening there was a surprise waiting. As I walked up the garden path I could hear a sort of noise – a bit like someone was trapped in a box with a gag on. Once I got into the hallway the noise got louder. Mum came out of the front room looking stressed.

"Oh, there you are," she said as if she'd been looking for me. Then she walked straight past me into the kitchen.

"Mmmm mmm mmm," said a voice from the front

room. I started to wonder if old age had finally caught up with Dulcie.

We don't normally go into the front room. Only if someone comes round who's the sort of person who has to have tea in a teapot.

Nervously I opened the door.

Nine

Dulcie was sitting on the settee looking happily at a little dog. It was exactly the same as Confucius, except that this one was dark brown.

It's actually quite hard to describe Pekinese dogs. They're not like real dogs, who have smaller tails than the rest of their bodies. With Dulcie's Pekinese it was hard to say where the tail ended and the body began. Its fur started on its back and came down to the ground in all directions. It had a squashy little black nose, which was really close to its eyes, so it looked snobby and cross, and its ears were big and silky.

When it saw me it went "mm mm mmm" even louder and ran round and round in circles before spiralling off behind the settee.

Dulcie said, "I'd like you to meet Nemesis. Nemesis dear, come and say hello to Jordan."

Nemesis looked snobbily at me and said, "MMMM!"

I sat down and tried to stroke her, but she bit my fingers.

"Nemesis dear!" said Dulcie sternly.

"Whose is she?" I asked.

"She's mine," said Dulcie calmly.

I gave her a nervous look. Dad had told us all that no one could ever have a pet because they cost money and do their business everywhere. Now I came to think of it, Dulcie had mentioned getting a pet before and there had been a pretty bad argument.

He did once let me and Joanna have some gerbils. They were called Mustaveadonut and Mustaveajammydodger. Unfortunately Mustaveadonut did actually eat Mustaveajammydodger. We know he ate him because Mustaveajammydodger's tail was hanging out of his mouth in the morning. Joanna cried for about three days and Mum said she was "absolutely traumatized". Dad went round the house saying in a jolly voice, "Oops, must 'ave a Jammy Dodger." Every time he said this Joanna screamed and hid in her room.

We had to give Mustaveadonut away. I'm afraid that after what happened no one could bear to look at him. Mum told his new owners he was a bit nervous around other pets and liked to be on his own, which is a grown-up way of saying he was a psychopath.

Joanna appeared in the doorway.

"Oh, isn't she gorgeous?" She opened her mouth and made her eyes really big.

"Her name's Nemesis," I told her.

"Oh, that's gorgeous," she said again.

I was hoping she'd get bitten, but, "She seems to like you." Dulcie sounded surprised.

Joanna said, "I have a way with animals? Once there was this injured horse? I was with Collette." (Collette is Joanna's, equally vile best friend.) "She was really nervous and it wouldn't let her go anywhere near? But I think it sensed that I was really calm and sort of – like it could trust me?"

At that point there was a noise that shut even Joanna up: Dad, taking his boots off in the hall! We looked nervously at Nemesis. She must have sensed danger because she stared at the door and started to rock from side to side.

When I first saw Nemesis rocking I thought it was a sign of fear. Now I know it means she's going to attack. Like when she met Confucius for the first time. (You'd have thought they would have wanted to be friends, but there you go.) Anyway you have to admire her bravery. As soon as Dad opened the door she glided across the floor like a terrible ghost dog and the next thing we knew Dad was going, "Arghh, arghh, it's a rat! It's a rat!" and Nemesis had her fangs locked into his neck.

Dulcie stood up creakily. "Dominic," she pulled feebly at Nemesis's tail, "you're making it worse. Ne-me-sis!" she said in a singing voice. "Naughty girl."

"Gmmmmm," said Nemesis.

"It's punctured my ******* jugular," shouted Dad, who had gone bright red.

Mum appeared in the doorway with a washing-up bowl full of water. "I knew this would happen," she said tiredly, and threw the lot at Nemesis, Dad and Dulcie.

Looking back, I think it's something she would probably have liked to do more often.

The next day at school I told Boy Dave and Ryan about it.

"It was the *hugest* row," I said. "Dad said Dulcie has to go and live in Sunset Villas and take Nemesis with her. Only obviously he didn't call her Nemesis – more like rat-mongrel, flea-bitten toerag, manky bog brush and other stuff. Mum and Joanna cried."

Boy Dave nodded supportively. "They always make a big thing of it, don't they? It's because they have really boring lives – they have to make a big crisis out of little things."

Ryan said, "It probably wasn't the best choice of dog for your dad either. If she'd chosen a Staffordshire bull terrier I expect he'd have got on really well with it."

"That depends," I said gloomily, "if it'd been a Staff he might be dead by now."

"Cool dogs, though," said Boy Dave, "Staffs."

We carried on talking about different dogs for a bit and it helped me not to worry. I didn't want Dulcie to have to go in a home and I didn't like it when Mum cried. I'd even felt a bit sorry for Joanna because, although I don't think she minded about Dulcie, she obviously really liked Nemesis.

Breakfast that morning had been terrible. No one talked to each other and Dad stomped off on his own to the cafe instead of sitting with us. I suppose it was the first time it had ever been like that when it wasn't my fault. Looking back I should have enjoyed it while I had the chance.

Ten

After break that day we all had to put on our art shirts and go to a part of the playground round the back of the new science lab. Not a lot happens there; there's just a long brick wall, where The Agnetha was lurking. To tell the truth, what with all the problems at home, I'd almost forgotten about the whole TV thing.

"Hi there, team," she said enthusiastically as we all traipsed round the corner. "Now, tell me, what do you see? Just a boring, empty wall, right? Well, I don't know about you, but I think it needs livening up a little?" A bit surprisingly she started handing out cans of spray paint. "Did you ever imagine that? Somewhere you can express yourselves without getting into trouble? Go ahead, make your mark! You can put whatever you want, as long as your message is positive and not unkind."

Me, Boy Dave and Ryan had already decided that spray-can graffiti wasn't for us. It's basically one of those things that looks really easy until you try it yourself. Then it ends up being this huge big mess that doesn't look like anything, and for weeks afterwards you have to pick untold amounts of gunky, multicoloured snot out of your nose. Some people are really good at it (the graffiti, not the nose-picking – though they probably get pretty slick at that as well) but I think they prefer to try and get their tag on really visible or hard to get to places like trains and bridges. I wasn't sure that a "special wall" in the school playground was exactly the same buzz.

"Go right ahead," said The Agnetha to me as I shook my can pathetically, "make your mark."

I sighed and sprayed an orange splodge next to Boy Dave's blue one.

"That's great, it looks like a bright orange sun. So hopeful. Why don't you choose another colour and try again."

"Look," I told her politely, "I've done the orange. That's all I feel like doing right now."

Luckily, at that moment, Connor accidentally sprayed himself lime green.

After about twenty minutes, when the wall was covered in badly drawn hearts and splodges and we were all feeling a bit dizzy from the paint fumes, The Agnetha clapped her hands. "OK, put your cans back in the box and follow me back to the classroom."

"Here we go," said Boy Dave tiredly. "If it's teddies we're out of there, OK?"

But back in class The Agnetha put on a serious face.

"Have a guess at the worst sort of emotion there is to carry around with you?" she asked.

"Being sad?" someone suggested.

"Jealous?" said someone else.

"Both of those are really tough emotions to have," agreed The Agnetha. "But how do they come out in the end?" She looked meaningfully round the room. "Anger! We get angry, don't we? So our problem is: how do we let go of all that negative anger?"

"Punch someone?" suggested the new-look Connor.

"Hmm," said The Agnetha. "But wouldn't it be great if we could do it in a way which doesn't hurt anyone? Why don't we try it? No, no," she said hastily, "NOT punching. I want you all to pretend that the person opposite you is someone or something you are really angry with. Go ahead, shout at them, scream; let it go."

We stared at the people opposite us in silence.

"Come on," said The Agnetha. "What would you like to say to that person that made you so angry?"

Rhajni Singh suddenly glared at me. "You know, you make me so mad when you take my things from my room."

I was about to say I'd never been near her room, but then I realized she'd actually decided to take part in the game.

All along the line little cross murmurs were

52

beginning. I looked over at Boy Dave for support, but he was staring at Steven Longacre, who was saying how much he hated the way Boy Dave never took him fishing.

People's faces started to go red and the noise got louder and louder. They yelled that the others were pigs and they hated them and there was quite a bit of swearing. But The Agnetha was gazing happily up at the silver ball and didn't seem to have noticed.

"ANGRY, ANGRY, ANGRY." Ryan suddenly leaped on to a desk and started jumping island-style towards the door. "ANGRY, ANGRY, ANGRY. I'm going to have to LEAVE."

"Me too," I said quickly.

"And me," said Boy Dave.

Once we were safely out of sight of the classroom we checked for cameras and microphones. By now there weren't many blind spots left in the building and in the end we hunched into a doorway.

"What was that meant to be?" said Boy Dave. His eyes were all starey. "Poppy Lockhart told Daniel Penfold she was going to cut out his tongue."

Ryan asked, "Am I the only one who thinks that all this stuff with The Agnetha isn't exactly as it seems?"

"How do you mean?"

"Well, I dunno. She seems more interested in how things are going to look on film than anything else."

"That's true," I agreed. "Even when people started

really swearing she was just looking up at the camera."

It was starting to get a bit uncomfortable being squidged up in the doorway between Boy Dave and Ryan (who, being an absent-minded sort of person, quite often doesn't bother with day-to-day things like washing, and can be a bit smelly).

"There must be somewhere else we can go," I said, trying to wriggle myself a bit more space.

Boy Dave shook his head. "Where? Those cameras are everywhere. The only thing we could do would be to bunk right out of school and even then we'd probably be caught on film."

"Well, we can't stay here. Anyway, I don't suppose they have time to look at all the films, they probably only watch the ones with The Agnetha in them."

Ryan poked his head round from the doorway and peered up at the ceiling.

"I could probably disable that one up there, if I reached over from the stairs."

Risking a look myself, I saw what he meant. Most of the cameras were too high, but it would be quite easy to get at this one if we climbed over the banister.

"Even if we just put something over it," I suggested, "at least we could sit on the stairs and wait for break. It's a shame we don't have any of the spray paint or we could do what bank robbers do and spray it."

In the end we settled for an art shirt. We flopped

down on the stairs, relieved to be just sitting down again, but it didn't last long. Almost straight away we heard footsteps coming from the landing above.

There wasn't enough time to get back in the doorway, so we hid behind the end of the lockers. A few moments later a podgy man with a beard and a woolly cardigan with white bobbles on it started down the stairs. It was as if he knew exactly what he was looking for because halfway down the stairs he stopped. Mumbling something under his breath he reached over, untangled the shirt from the camera, and dropped it on the floor. Then he turned and headed back off up the stairs again.

We looked at each other. It was weird that he seemed to know exactly where to find the art shirt, but it was weird for another reason as well.

Our school is like three boxes stuck together: the original main school where most of the classrooms are; the gym; and the school theatre where we have assembly. As you go in the main entrance there's a staircase in the middle of the hall that leads up to the vending machine. At the top is a long balcony going along on the right, which overlooks the gym. At the end of that is another staircase, which comes down again on the other side of the classrooms. The school theatre is also at the other end, but the door to get into the theatre is downstairs. Basically there was nowhere for the man to go – unless he was going to walk along the balcony and just come back down the stairs on the other side.

But there was no time to worry about it. A sudden hiss/crackle made us jump. Bobble man reached down, unclipped a walkie-talkie from his belt and held it to his ear. We couldn't hear what the voice at the other end said, but Bobble said, "Roger that."

Then slowly he turned and stared right at the end of the lockers where we were peeping round.

Eleven

It was like *Jack and the Beanstalk*, when the giant can smell Jack's blood. Bobble had known! He had known we were there. The crackly voice had told him. There was completely no expression on his face as he walked towards us and said, "You're not meant to be here."

Boy Dave and Ryan were already heading for the door and I raced after them. We took the entrance steps two at a time into the yard, and were about to make the final dash for the school gates when the worst thing that could have happened, happened.

The fire alarm went off.

Even then we might have made it, but a dark figure was already marching across the yard: Jefferson was on his way with his stopwatch to time the fire drill.

Like a shoal of fish, me, Boy Dave and Ryan swerved round at exactly the same time and bolted back up the steps. Bobble might be a blank-faced contract killer who had been sent to deal with us once and for all, but charging straight towards him was way safer than charging straight towards Jefferson.

"Oof!" went Bobble as we passed him in the doorway.

"YOU BOYS!" bellowed the voice of a maniac behind us.

People had started spilling out of the classrooms and it was really crowded in the hallway. Everyone was surging towards us, trying to get out into the yard for the drill, but the only tiny chance we had was to go in the opposite direction. We had learned from a few unfortunate problems last year that if we could get to the stairs we might be able to make it along the balcony, down the other side and away. We might even be in time to line up for the fire register and pretend it wasn't us.

Shoving and elbowing, we pushed our way through the crowd, while a little way behind, Jefferson and Bobble tried to do the same. Jefferson had a huge advantage because people actually tried to get out of his way, but he must have been a bit held up because we managed to make it as far as the stairs.

As we raced up them we could hear him yelling above a big sea of noise from the hallway, but once we were on the balcony it was strangely quiet. The only sounds were our trainers squeaking, and the muffled ringing of the fire bell below.

It didn't last:

"YOU BOYS! GET 'ERE NOW."

There was the loud crash of the door smashing

open behind us. At triple-speed we banged through the doors at our end and were just about to bomb down the back staircase, when Boy Dave yanked my sleeve,

"Wait! Wait."

He was pointing to a door at the top of the stairs. We tended to forget about this door. Inside is a small room, with a huge glass window, which looks down on the stage, where they do assembly. They operate the sound and lighting for school plays from there, but it's out of bounds and is nearly always locked. Unusually, on that day, though, the door was half open. Maybe whoever was in there had heard the fire alarm and left in a hurry.

Quick as a flash me, Boy Dave and Ryan piled in and slammed the door shut behind us. Not even a second later we heard the double doors on the landing bang again and the sound of Jefferson's boots clomping down the back staircase.

It wasn't until the sound had completely died away that we actually started to breathe again and look around. But, when we saw what was in there, our mouths dropped open. And after that we just stood dead still and stared.

Twelve

"Wow," whispered Boy Dave at last. "It's like being God."

The whole left side of the room was covered in screens. Rows and rows of them, as high as the ceiling. It was just like on television when they're meant to be monitoring security, except these were colour. Even just standing there made you feel powerful.

Underneath each screen was a number: one for the gym; the canteen; some parts of the playground; the hallway.

"That's our classroom," I looked at the eerily empty desks, "forty-seven B."

"Those must be the camera numbers," said Ryan. "There's a laptop here, on the control panel. Oh!"

"Blimey!" Boy Dave bent down and squinted at the image. "It's us. What are we doing?"

"It's a movie," said Ryan. "Hang on, I'll rewind it."

"No," a small flicker of movement on the screens above caught my eye, "wait." Three men were coming along the back corridor and heading for the stairs. One of them was Bobble. "We'd better get out of here," I said urgently.

But we should have realized that once Ryan was in there it would be impossible to get him out again. His eyes, which had sort of glazed over, were reflecting the little multicoloured lights on the control panel as if his head was filled with them.

"I think we should stay for a while and watch," he said, nodding massively as if he was trying to hypnotize us.

"No. What if we get caught?" I shook his arm. "What if they're here 24-7 and we can't get out again?"

But it was too late. According to the image on screen the men were already on the back staircase. If we went out of the door now, they would see us for sure.

The only good place to hide was underneath the sound desk on the opposite side of the room from the screens. It wasn't great: there were loads of thick, dangling-down, dusty cables and if anyone moved the big leather swivel chair in front they would see us for sure.

We crouched as near to the back as possible and held our breath as three men walked into the room.

"Right," said the first man. He was wearing a faded T-shirt with that old-fashioned Crazy Frog on it and a battered-looking black leather jacket. "Where were we?"

Bobble sat down next to him and flicked the mouse on the laptop. It was a film of our class jumping on the desks.

"Totally out-of-control kids," said the Crazy Frog Man. "Now splice in the teacher trying to restore order."

Up came Miss Fairjoy talking and waving her arms around. Beside me Boy Dave went, "Uhhh?"

There hadn't even been a teacher there when we were doing Islands and Sharks.

"Now the abuse," said Crazy Frog Man.

It was our class yelling at each other and swearing.

"Nice. Now the teacher again."

This time it was Mr Fern, banging his fist on the wall and storming about. "Why, man, he doth bestride the narrow world," he was saying angrily. "Like a Colossus, and we petty men walk under his huge legs and peep about to find ourselves dishonourable graves."

"What's he saying?" asked the Crazy Frog Man.

"Ermmm some drama thing," mumbled Bobble.

"Can we drown that out with an overdub of the kids?"

The other man, who looked like Shaggy out of Scooby Doo, came over and sat down. He moved to a grey-looking page on the computer and pushed up a virtual sound control. On another page, he moved around a few wiggly lines. When the image of Fern came back, it really was like he was trying to yell at a load of kids and his voice was being drowned out by shouting and swearing.

"Right," said Crazy Frog Man, "can we get one of the illegal-chocolate-selling kids vandalizing the school?"

My eyes almost fell out of their sockets. It was me looking really fed up. I was spraying an orange splodge on the wall.

The Crazy Frog Man tutted and sat back. "It needs more," he said. "Sort of like a main theme to it."

"There's, mmmumble, not a lot to go on," mumbled Shaggy.

"Never is," said the Crazy Frog Man. "We want kids she can actually cure or there's no programme."

Above, on screen forty-seven B our class was settling back down for lessons. Even if we managed to get out of there we were going to be in massive trouble.

Suddenly the Crazy Frog Man started laughing. "Look – hothead fifty-seven A. That army bloke's making them clean all the graffiti off."

It was Jefferson with some of year nine. They had buckets and brushes and he was making them scrub the wall. The two other blokes started snuffling, which I later found out was their way of laughing.

"Crazy." The Crazy Frog Man shook his head. Then he went thoughtful for a bit and the other two ate their sandwiches.

Soon after that the Crazy Frog Man went off somewhere, but Shaggy and Bobble stayed, pottering about and messing with the computer. It was terrible. It felt as if we had been under that sound desk for weeks. We had pins and needles and could hardly breathe for dust.

There was one hopeful moment when they started clearing away the coffee cups and food wrappers, but it turned out they were just making room for the chessboard.

Thirteen

"Hmm," said the man who looked like Shaggy. "Interesting. *En passant.*"

Boy Dave put both his hands over his face and whimpered. After ten minutes of complete stillness and silence Bobble had finally moved a piece. By the time they actually finished their chess game the rest of the human race would have evolved into pink brains in glass boxes linked to computers and robots. We would be freaks in an unknown, distant future.

Nervously I moved some of the cables to one side and peered along the back of the sound desk. The door was only a few feet along, but it was tightly closed. We could probably crawl to it without too many problems – there was enough noise coming from the screens to cover us and we would be hidden for most of the way by the sound desk – but there was no way we could open it and get out without them knowing. On the other hand. . .

I tapped Boy Dave and Ryan and pointed to say I was going to crawl along but Ryan shook his head violently. "Trust me," I whispered.

I pushed aside the heavy cables and inched along until I was right at the edge of the sound desk. By now I was almost close enough to reach out and touch the door.

The two men were still staring down at their game. On the screens above were distant images of school going on as usual and I got that cold feeling you get when you know you're going to be in real trouble: we had to get out of there.

Urged on by the thought of actually eating and drinking again (not to mention going to the toilet), I took a deep breath and judged the distance between where I was crouched and the door. *One*, I said to myself, *two...*

I threw myself at the door and wrenched open the handle before slamming it again really loudly as though I'd just dashed in. Then I stood staring at the men. "Oh," I said, "sorry. Wrong room."

Bobble looked up dozily. "You're mmmnnnot allowed in here," he mumbled.

"Are you the television people?" I asked. "Only I saw some kids with, like, spray cans. They were going to spray some of the cameras."

Bobble and Shaggy carried on looking dozy.

"Really big kids," I said, jumping up and down, trying to get some energy into them. "They were down in the hall."

Bobble wiggled a knob on his control panel. "There's no one there."

"They're hiding behind the lockers. They put an art shirt over it earlier on. Come on, quickly, I'll show you."

With a sad, loving look at the chessboard he got to his feet.

"You'd better both come," I said, jumping wildly, "they've all got huge puffa jackets on for protection and . . . and also they're *hoodies* and they look really violent. One of them has his whole face tattooed lime green."

It nearly, *almost*, worked, but at that moment (and I don't know who it was – Ryan and Boy Dave have been blaming each other ever since) the sound desk let out an enormous fart.

"It was the angry stuff," explained Ryan to the headmistress. "We just felt so angry we had to run away."

The head raised her eyebrows at The Agnetha, who shook her head and said, "Fascinating," in a creepy voice.

"Going into places that are out of bounds. Missing fire drill. Truancy," said the head sternly. "This is extremely serious."

"Just a moment." The Agnetha held up a hand. She turned to us and said in a kind voice, "It's OK, you can share it with me. You were scared, weren't you? Scared of your own anger."

After a confused moment we nodded sadly. The

Agnetha turned to the head. "Role play is so powerful. It obviously stirred up some really painful feelings for these young men. Am I right?" she asked us gently.

We nodded more sadly.

"You know," she explained, "behind every disruptive pupil there's a really scared little child just waiting to come out. Tell me: how did all this sudden anger welling up inside make you feel?"

"Scared," we said, "really scared."

"Honestly,' said Boy Dave, as we finally walked home. "They're up in that little room, making out we're all vandals and swearing all the time and then she comes in and saves us from destruction and says we're all cute little guys. . ."

"That was the bears," I reminded him.

"Huh, I'm beginning to think she doesn't know the difference."

"Oh no." I suddenly had a worrying thought. "I really hope she doesn't start hugging us. I think it's, like, her religion."

Ryan coughed and ate another handful of fizzy colas, which is all we'd managed to get to eat since breakfast.

"Well, it's not really as contradictory as it might seem. The Crazy Frog man pretty much said they want us all to look really bad and totally out of control, then The Agnetha can cure us with love and understanding. Abracadabra."

Boy Dave frowned. "Why don't they pick on all Joanna's lot? They're dying to be in it."

We'd reached the edge of Hangman's Lane and it was time for Boy Dave to peel off up to his house.

"Before you go." Ryan handed Boy Dave an envelope. He tapped it meaningfully. "A matter of vital importance. You will find the details of the operation enclosed therein. Memorize and destroy." Then he gave one to me too.

Obviously Ryan's handouts were destined to go the way of all handouts, and get mixed up with a load of crumbs and sticky stuff at the bottom of our schoolbags and probably eventually rot away, so, once we'd said goodbye to Boy Dave, I asked, "What's in the handout?"

Ryan took a deep, serious breath. "A highly detailed blueprint of how we are to become the first humans to welcome aliens to planet earth."

I smiled at the thought. It was becoming a really nice, clear evening and the air smelled of the last of summer – flowers and earth – and the birds were singing. The idea of doing one of Ryan's projects had cheered me up and I started to feel as if all that reality TV stuff had just been a kind of stressful, hungry-making bad dream. After all, from now on we would just make sure we didn't have anything to do with them and, sooner or later, they would all go away again and things would be back to normal.

Fourteen

On Wednesday, apart from a few distant sightings, we didn't see much of The Agnetha, but that Thursday we were just going into the gym, when we heard a familiar foreign-sounding voice heartily going, "Welcome, team."

Which was pretty sneaky, because even we wouldn't have thought she could take over Jefferson's PE lesson.

We had a quick look down from the balcony just to make sure that Jefferson and The Agnetha hadn't teamed up together (which, let's face it, was pretty unlikely), but it was just her.

She was making one person run as fast as they could with a blindfold on while someone else had to catch them before they cracked their head on the vault horse. This was called a "trust game".

We later heard there had been another one where you had to fall backwards into someone's arms. Emma was meant to be catching Poppy but at the last minute she went, "She's too big, she's too big," and completely dropped her and they fell out for the rest of the week. All I can say is I don't know how anyone ever had the cheek to ban us from playing "dizzy" with the hockey stick.

Once we were safely out of the school we took the back lanes down to the garden centre. People who go there are normally outsiders who have driven in, and not spies from the village, so it's quite good for hopping school. As we got near the entrance a man came out of a small white tent and gave us each a balloon with *Silverstone's Garden Centre* written on it.

"Special promotion," he said. "Tell your mums and dads: four bags of compost for twelve pounds."

We spent the next half hour crouching under the table in the gnome section. Whenever someone walked past we breathed in some of the helium from the balloons and said in helium gnome-type voices, "Choose me, choose me. No, take me."

On our way back to school for dinner we noticed that the promotion man had left the balloons tied outside.

There aren't really that many uses for a large bunch of helium balloons (unless you want to pretend you're a gnome for life or send little airborne messages to unknown people), but it's one of those things – the same as when my mum buys really gross, wrong-size clothes in the sales – a big bunch of helium balloons is a sort of bargain not to be missed. And, as it happened, on the way back to school, we did actually think of a very good use for them.

Fifteen

I think it was what we did to the cuddly toys which upset everyone.

We found that if we tied one of The Agnetha's little guys to about five balloons, they floated along at eye height and, instead of getting stuck on the ceiling, the balloons got seriously in the way of the cameras. Some people who had actually chosen the little guys tried to make out it was like voodoo and took it all far too personally. And Miss Fairjoy said they were macabre. But, as we pointed out, "Whoever did this terrible thing probably just logically found tying the strings round the necks was the best way to get them airborne." (I must admit the fact that Ryan had already taken off the eyes "for future use", and was keeping them in a creepy sort of starey jam jar probably didn't help – but that was just coincidence.)

At afternoon break we were sitting on one of the benches in the school playground having a few sneaky bars of chocolate, when we noticed that the headmistress had braved the searing agony of daylight and come into the school yard. She was standing over by the school gates talking to The Agnetha and, rather worryingly, they were looking in our direction. After a bit The Agnetha broke away and charged at us before we had time to escape.

"Hi," she said. "Now, let me see if I can get this right." She pointed at each one of us in turn. "Jordan, David and Ryan." She'd got us all in the wrong order. "I've heard quite a bit about you guys."

Boy Dave said, "We'd probably better be getting back to lessons."

We stood up and she did her Eskimo-teeth smiley thing.

"It can be quite hard knowing what to say to grown-ups who are friendly for a change," she said knowingly.

Ryan stuck his neck forward to inspect her, like he does with dragonflies. "That's actually quite clever. You think we're used to grown-ups being rude to us, so we always start off by being rude, then when you're polite to us we don't really know what to do."

For a moment The Agnetha did look a bit like one of his jar creatures.

I said, "To be honest, most grown-ups normally do start off by being quite friendly to us."

Boy Dave said, "We don't really like it. We prefer to keep things separate."

"How do you mean separate, Jordan?" she asked Boy Dave.

He shrugged. "Em . . . like you should probably find someone your own age to talk to."

She shook her head wonderingly. "I am so looking forward to working with you amazing young men."

"As a matter of fact," said Ryan firmly, "I'm afraid we're not going to be taking part in it any more."

"It's probably the upsetting angry thing," I told her, remembering what Mum had said about the gerbils. "We were absolutely traumatized."

"And is that why you did what you did with the toy animals?" asked The Agnetha, sitting down on the bench. "To show me that you thought I was to blame for your distress?"

"Animals?" we asked.

"Yes!" she said sternly. "What *you* did with the animals and balloons."

"We don't know anything about that," Boy Dave told her nicely.

"I have a piece of film which says that you do," said The Agnetha, also nicely. Then she went serious. "Listen to me, I can help you, but only if you let me. It's only a few days into term and you kids are already in big trouble. Wouldn't it be better to work with me on how we can turn this negative behaviour around before it's too late?"

"Why?" asked Boy Dave. "Just so you can go making programmes that aren't even. . ." I nudged him hard. "Very good," he finished lamely.

"It was really your fault," I reminded her. "Your powerful thing made us scared of our anger. And apart from that it's just a few balloons, which wasn't even us."

"That stuff with the soft toys really gives me cause for concern." She frowned. "You know, you boys need help before this escalates."

"And you really give me cause for concern," said Ryan crossly.

We stood up and started to walk off, but The Agnetha got up and stood in front of us.

"We know it was you three who did that sick thing with the cuddly toys that you stole from me." Funnily enough, the way her face had gone suddenly red and angry-looking reminded me of Jefferson. "You guys need to think seriously about your futures. I mean that. You should take my offer of help while you still have the chance."

A little way off the head was still waiting. The Agnetha looked over at her and said loudly, "Now, you boys, just remember," as if we'd gone along with everything she wanted, "next time you feel the urge to do something bad, you just say *No to Mr Negative*. You hear me?" She wagged a finger at us. "*No to Mr Negative*."

"Do you think she believes this Mr Negative really exists?" I asked as we stared after her. "Or is it like a little sort of puppet that she gets out of a special box, like, 'say hello to Mr. Negative, everyone'?"

"Yeah," said Boy Dave, "but then Mr Negative turns evil and murders the whole school one by one."

"No, that would be her; Mr Negative would just tell her what to do from his box. His eyes would go round and he would say: *You know what to do*, and she would go: *No, no, don't make me do it again*."

Ryan said boringly, "It's a kind of psychology. They think if they get you to say 'no' to a sort of imaginary Mr Negative in your head, then, after a bit, you won't be able to do the stuff they don't want you to do. It's like brainwashing."

"You can't be brainwashed unless you want to be," said Boy Dave confidently.

"Actually," Ryan looked at him over the top of his glasses, "if you're exposed to it enough, you can. It's like some religious sects, they start off being really nice and friendly and people get to really like it and think it's great. Then, gradually they cut them off from their families and friends until the person totally depends on the others in the sect. That's when they start to really brainwash them and the person doesn't even know it's happening."

I had a sudden flashback to our class all getting to their feet in order to give each other a great big hug.

"Do you think that's what she's doing?" I asked worriedly. "Gradually brainwashing everyone?"

"I think it's very possible. She may even be an FBI agent who's been sent to stop us. They were probably monitoring hits to alien websites and have sent her to brainwash us before we can make contact with other intelligent life forms. But she will fail in her mission. Now, more than ever, it's vital that we continue our work."

Sixteen

Ryan's mum is an artist and she has a big barn which she uses as a studio where we quite often meet. By eleven that Saturday we were all round there and Ryan was giving us our instructions. Her latest painting was on the easel. It looked a bit like how Dulcie's trainspotter friend might have looked in his last moments.

"It's called *Explosion of Intricate Farrago*," explained Ryan.

"What's the plan?" I was impatient to get on with something a bit more interesting.

Ryan suddenly went pointy and businesslike. "Right, I've copied you both off some information about the project." He handed us each a printout, with a few blurred photographs of aliens and other stuff, which we were never likely to read. "And I've prepared the kit." He pulled a large cardboard box out from underneath an old trestle table. "This item is of particular interest." He extracted a sort of rusty barrel-shaped thing with a handle. "It's an old air raid siren."

Boy Dave and I started to feel excited. Ryan had obviously thought it all out really well.

"These here will define the landing pad in case they actually want to land tonight." He pulled out a string of multicoloured garden lights. "One small thing is – I can't help thinking we're going to need something really bright."

"We could let off some fireworks," I suggested.

Ryan looked doubtful. "They're used to seeing those. They'll probably just think it's someone's birthday. I was thinking of more like an old searchlight. You know, like they used to have in the war. Obviously we can't get hold of one of those, but I was really after something with a parabolic reflector."

I should say at this point that Ryan's favourite subject is science, which sometimes makes him a bit difficult to understand.

"A what?" said Boy Dave.

"It's how car headlights work," Ryan explained. "It's a curved metal cup which makes the light beams go into parallel rays and stops them scattering."

"Well, that's easy," I said. "We can just get the headlights off our dads' vans and use those."

Ryan shook his head. "I think we're going to need quite a few. On the other hand, we could have a go at making our own. I imagine," he looked thoughtfully at the *Explosion of Intricate Farrago*, "that if we placed enough light sources into a curved metal container, we could make something that resembled an old searchlight."

Boy Dave and me hadn't really thought aliens would land at all, or even notice us, but after everything that had happened at school, anything was worth a try, and anyway, having something to do helped take our minds off it a bit. Also, we didn't want to offend Ryan and we both thought the bright-light idea was a really good one.

"Right," said Boy Dave briskly, "what can we use?"

It took us a long time to come up with the right parts but I think it was worth the effort. Because the light was going to be shining upwards, we decided we could just as well get away with a metal dustbin but with something curved at the bottom. That way, Ryan explained, the light would be harnessed and focused upwards and the sides of the bin would make sure it didn't escape.

None of us wanted to use our own satellite dishes because we all like TV, so we decided the best one to get would be Andy's from the Black Horse.

"I'll get a pair of wire cutters from Dad's tool kit," said Boy Dave. "I'll go down on site and pretend Mum asked me to give him a sandwich."

"But you won't have a sandwich," I pointed out.

"Yes I will," said Boy Dave confidently. "I'll just make it myself."

Ryan and me looked at each other doubtfully.

"I've got a better idea," I said. "Tell him that Andy from the Black Horse asked if he could borrow some tools to get down his old satellite dish. That way he'll give you exactly the right ones."

Boy Dave looked thoughtful. "As a matter of fact, that's not a bad idea."

I tried not to look pleased.

"We'll also have to get hold of loads of lamps and stuff," said Ryan.

"Hang on a minute," I realized in the excitement of it all that we didn't even know where all this was to take place, "will there be places to plug them all in?"

Ryan polished his glasses on his jumper. He always does this when he's feeling a bit clever.

"We actually only need one power point. Then we just need a system of extension leads and suchlike."

"By the way," I said, "where exactly are the aliens going to land?"

Ryan popped his glasses back on. Behind them his eyes gleamed a bit madly. "There is only one suitable place," he said. "The roof of the new science lab."

Seventeen

It was quite easy after that. Boy Dave's dad had given him exactly the right tools to get the satellite dish down and no one seemed to have noticed. By the time they all wanted to watch the football in the back bar we were long gone. We decided to borrow the bin from school and I personally managed to get two lamps from Mum and Dad's room, one each from Joanna and Dulcie and a couple from the living room. I reckoned, if we could all get five or six each, any alien who missed that was going to be too blind to ever land on planet earth and destroy it anyway.

It didn't get dark until around eight thirty but we agreed to meet up earlier. Also, there was a chance that someone might just want to put a lamp on in our houses by evening and then they would find out that there weren't any left, so they would immediately blame us and make a big fuss. There was also quite a lot of preparation to do. Luckily it was the night of the summer concert and in our house we were eating early.

I could smell the vinegar as I walked in. We

normally only ever have fish and chips on Friday. Dad secretly likes fish and chips but he pretends it's second best because it's not home-cooked by Mum. But sure enough there were mine, keeping warm in the oven. I splashed a big dollop of ketchup on them and went through to the living room. It was a weird atmosphere.

"Why are we having fish and chips?" I asked, pulling out a chair at the table, where everyone was sitting really quietly.

Mum said quickly, "Hasn't it been a glorious day?'

But Dad said, "We were meant to be having steak," and looked at Dulcie across the table.

Dulcie said, "When we were rationed in the war my mother used to make do with half a tin of corned beef and powdered egg. As a matter of fact, I'm still very fond of corned beef and scrambled egg."

"Funnily enough," said Dad, putting on a silly voice, "I'm very fond of steak for my tea, but I can't have *steak* because some silly old bat has gone and fed it to some waste of space little rat dog what doesn't deserve it anyway."

Mum said, "Dominic, that is uncalled for."

Mum and Dad don't have that many rows because Dad doesn't know how to use the kitchen things. He can actually use the cooker a bit, but last time he and Mum had a row he got tired of eating bacon and food which was still a bit frozen. Also, he ran out of clean clothes and didn't know where anything was. He tried asking Joanna but she wasn't much help. When he asked where his not-washed-for-five-days T-shirt was she said, "Like, I think it's crawled away to die on its own?"

Point being he tries not to argue too badly with Mum. Also, to show he's properly sorry, she expects him to buy her flowers, which he finds embarrassing.

"All set for the concert, darling?" Mum asked Joanna.

Joanna made this great dramatic sigh and put her hands on her chest and tummy. "Like, I am sooo nervous. I mean everyone was really pleased with the dress rehearsal and my solo went really well, even though it's got a really difficult range? And I've got all these extra duties now because Danielle Romley is meant to have gastroenteritis, but, like, Collette saw her going to Brighton on the bus and she looked perfectly fine? And Collette said. . ."

It just went on and on. I started to think that as part of the "war on terror" we might be able to give Joanna to the Americans. Instead of playing terrorist suspects loud music, which isn't to their taste, she could tell them about the school concert.

By the time tea was over, Dad was trying to watch TV from the kitchen table and Dulcie had taken Nemesis into the garden to "get some air". Dad was in a really bad mood because of Dulcie refusing to take a plastic bag out with her, but there was no chance of having a proper argument because Joanna wouldn't let anyone else get a word in edgeways. By now she was standing up, walking round with her arms out at the sides like a Christmas tree, going, "...and then, after we've formed a circle shape, the girls at the front kind of make a dip and come backwards and the girls at the back kind of straighten out to make a point, so, like, we make a heart shape? Then the boys come and take the arms of the girls at the front, but there are actually only three boys? So some girls have to do it as well? And the heart parts gently and I come out like this," (weird hands-out-to-the-side walk) "and they all hold out an arm to greet me. Then I do my solo. . ."

I think, by this time, even Mum was starting to drift in and out of consciousness. She said, "Would you like to come with us to the concert tonight, Jordan?"

Joanna made a face like she'd just smelled dog poo (which wasn't a complete impossibility, what with Nemesis taking the night air and all). She said, "Do NOT bring him."

"Joanna," said Mum sternly, "Jordan might want to see the concert."

Dad suddenly looked jolly, which is always worrying. "Tell you what. You and Dulcie go and I'll take Jordan off for a couple of games of pool."

I felt nervous. We had big plans for that night but it

would be more than my life was worth to spoil Dad's chances of getting out of the concert. Luckily Mum raised her eyebrows in a particular way and Dad looked crushed.

"Well," he said grumpily, standing up, "me and Big Dave have got snagging to do." Which is his way of saying they're going down the pub.

"Back by six thirty," said Mum in the same voice as the eyebrows. "Did you want to see the concert, darling?" she asked me kindly.

I felt quite sorry for her. She always hopes I'll become the sort of person who would actually enjoy watching Joanna and her silly friends howling and writhing like a pit of demented vampires at sunrise.

"No thank you, Mum," I told her. "I'd rather drink a bucket of sick."

Joanna said, "Like, there are some really good children's homes nowadays?"

At that moment Dulcie came tottering in with Nemesis. Mum looked worried. "Dulcie, darling, dogs need more exercise than that. She'll get miserable."

Dulcie pretended not to have heard and said something vague about "going to draw a bath".

Poor Dulcie, she really wanted to have a pet, but it's true that she is quite doddery and slow and needs lots of rests.

"I'll take Nemesis out," I offered. "We were only going to hang round the Green anyway."

Mum looked at me suspiciously. "When you say hang round. . .?"

"Play football," I said hurriedly. "Nemesis would love it."

I think Dulcie was secretly quite happy that I was taking Nemesis with me, but she made out it was like a great big treat and gave me a huge long load of instructions about how exactly Nemesis should cross the road, and what temperature she had to have her coat on and blah blah. Then she made me fill up all my pockets with really stinky dog biscuits, which Nemesis was meant to be allowed if she sat "nicely". I decided that as soon as I got the chance I would give them all to her at once, like a sort of mini meal.

Eighteen

I should say at this point that Nemesis thoroughly enjoyed her start to the evening. We all climbed up (well, Nemesis was carried) on to the science-lab roof, then we ate a few bars of the mountain of chocolate we'd brought for the aliens as a peace offering. There were quite a few people about in the school yard below, on their way to the welcome concert – which was going to be on the playing field on the other side of the school, so we hid behind an air vent and surveyed the landing site.

"Do you think it'll actually be big enough?" Boy Dave asked Ryan.

He nodded. "Certainly. Some of the craft they've found in Arizona are very small reconnaissance ships. You could probably get about three on here."

Despite myself I felt really excited. After all, there was a chance they might come. I mean, looking at it another way, why shouldn't they? We'd gone to a lot of effort to show we meant business. I asked, "Which power point are we going to use?"

Ryan had managed to pinch his mum's computer

extension without her knowing. This had five power points on it, and he'd also got another lead which had five points as well. Boy Dave and I had managed to get another three extension leads between us all with two points each. By my reckoning, we were going to have at least thirteen lights going at once.

"You know that door which leads down to the bin cellar?" Ryan asked. "They never bother to lock it, and there's a plug in there." That's the sort of thing Ryan notices, he's a bit weird like that.

The bin cellar is right next door to the science lab, so it wasn't too much of a problem for Ryan to climb down and run an extension lead up from the basement. We had to use one of mine and Boy Dave's leads to begin with, which meant we wasted a power socket, but once we'd plugged Ryan's mum's one in it reached quite easily on to the landing site. The next thing was to get all the lamps into the parabolic reflector bin.

"The glass of the bulbs mustn't be touching," Ryan said sternly, "or there might be an accident."

It was pretty tricky, especially fitting Joanna's Justin Timberlake lampshade in, which is an awkward shape, but by making a sort of light fountain, we managed to get eight altogether. We'd decided not to use mirrors, so we'd used a roll of my mum's tinfoil round the sides to reflect the light back into the bin.

I rolled out the garden lights while Boy Dave and

Ryan painted a sort of white star-shaped landing pad on the roof. Finally, we arranged the air raid siren on its stand.

"Whatever you do," said Ryan, "don't wind that handle up until the last minute."

Boy Dave eyed the rusty old barrel thing suspiciously. "Does it actually still work?"

"Oh yes," Ryan's eyes gleamed in the twilight, "it works."

When everything was ready we went to have a look at the concert. I won't go into detail because it's probably the most boring thing you would ever hear about in your life. Joanna's choir were all wearing long white dresses and standing on a sort of round stage thing in the middle of the school field, with all the mums and dads sat round pretending to enjoy it (and the new ones pretending to be impressed). The film crew were there as well, circling round near the front of the stage with a big furry microphone and camera on wheels. When it was Joanna's turn, she started doing little side steps to get in the shot and staring like a distressed cow into the camera. I got the impression the film crew had started doing little side steps to try and avoid her.

We hid on the bank down by the stream and Nemesis even had a little swim. The smell of autumn was hanging in the air. It reminded me that

Halloween was soon, then fireworks night, then, best of all, Christmas. The moon and stars were already bright, it was going to be a perfect night for aliens to land. We listened to the end of Poppy Lockhart's violin solo, which was like a small animal in dreadful pain, and then headed back. By then it was starting to get really dark.

I should say at this point that Ryan's parabolic bin was brilliant. It's hard to say how brilliant because it was so bright it was actually a bit painful to look at. The garden lights worked pretty well too, although, as Boy Dave pointed out, the spacecraft would actually squash them as it came down, but Ryan said by that time they would have served their purpose.

Looking back, I suppose it might have been better to wait until after the new parents' welcome concert. The school are ridiculously proud of their concerts, which normally end on a bit where the whole orchestra and choir all do everything at once and there is much cymbal clashing and cheering as the parents shout, "encore!", and someone gives cretacious Clark, the music teacher, a bunch of flowers, even though she is deaf and can only play six songs which are:

1. "Nymphs and Shepherds"
2. The, I closed my eyes (and went to sleep it was so boring) ahhahhahh one

3. "Jerusalem"
4. "Eleanor Rigby" by the Beatles
5. Some complete embarrassment called "Sweet Little Maids a Wandering"
6. "Onward Christian Soldiers"

Point being, the concert is obviously something that everyone involved finds far too exciting.

"Right," said Ryan. All you could see of him was a shadowy shape in the dark. "I think it's time to give the signal." And, like a crazed organ grinder, he began to turn the handle on the air raid siren.

Nineteen

I suppose the best way to describe the sound of an air raid siren is sad. It wails like a ghost but much louder and a bit lower. As the noise built and built and the lights shone brighter and brighter up into the night sky Boy Dave jumped excitedly.

"There they are!" he shouted. "Look, look!"

And there they were: lights circling interestedly in the sky, some red, some white. Definitely not like anything we'd ever seen before. We jumped up and down, madly waving our arms. "Here!" we cried. "We're here!"

"MM-MM-MM-MM-MM," went Nemesis, rushing round and round.

"Make them an offering of peace," yelled Ryan. "Throw out the chocolate."

Frantically I went through my pockets. Boy Dave did the same and then looked helplessly over at me. I shook my head. It seemed impossible, but we must have accidentally eaten all the offerings of peace. All I had left in my pockets were Nemesis's stinky dog biscuits.

The engines of the spaceship had become louder and it seemed to be hovering lower now. They were probably looking down on us right this minute, wondering whether to land. But without the chocolate how would they know it wasn't a trap? Maybe it had even happened before; that their friends had landed and walked straight out into armed guards and been shot. This was terrible. We had to find a way of showing that we were their friends.

Desperately I tried my pockets again, but there was nothing.

Then I had a sudden thought: OK – *we* liked chocolate. But we were humans. There was nothing to say that aliens liked it. In fact, there was no way of knowing what aliens liked to eat. *In fact*, in some ways, it seemed quite likely that they might prefer something more . . . *dry*, and strong-smelling. Chances were they probably really enjoyed the sort of food that we humans found revolting!

Quickly I grabbed a handful of Nemesis's biscuits and threw them up into the beam of light.

"Look," I shouted, grabbing more and more handfuls and throwing them about wildly, "look, food for you. Food!"

We could feel the rush of air as the craft hovered lower; hear the chugging of advanced technology faintly above the sound of the air raid siren as it went *oo-oo-oo* up and down mournfully.

Our hearts were banging, and our throats hurt from all the shouting.

Then something strange happened. There was a quick fizzing noise, a sort of longish bang, some orange sparks like you would normally never see, and then, a little bit further away, only the lights of the spaceship were left, with the moon pale behind them.

"They've taken the lights," I shouted excitedly, pointing at the sky. "The aliens have got our lights!"

But Boy Dave and Ryan were crouched over, looking at something.

I could see Ryan's lips moving but, even though the air raid siren had stopped, there was a loud ringing in my ears, so I couldn't hear what he was saying. I walked over and looked down to where he was pointing.

It was a huge smoking crater in the roof. Far down below was the parabolic reflector. The extension flex was hanging through the hole with some of the lamps still dangling and there was a smell like burnt rubber.

When we stood up and turned round, we saw white dresses from the choir like flying ghosts, rushing across the field and the playground in all different directions.

There were a few people standing right below the landing pad as well: Jefferson, the headmistress, the local policeman – PC White. And the television crew.

I don't know if there's some law against being made to stand in the school gym with a maniac shouting, "I'll ask you one more time: NAME. RANK. NUMBER."

Jefferson would most probably have known who we were on a normal day, but his army training means he gets a bit over-involved in things.

Ryan said, "Marconi. Lance Corporal WD40."

Jefferson looked pleased with himself and walked round him a couple of times. "Who sent you?"

"Sergeant major, sir," said Ryan, "I am to tell you that all birds fly south in winter." Boy Dave was nudging Ryan frantically but there was no stopping him.

"And the aim of your mission?" Jefferson poked Ryan with the end of a hockey stick, then batted Nemesis, who was trying to get some dog biscuits, which had somehow got into his hair.

"Amber-rated sergeant major," said Ryan. "Code name Madagascar." He tapped the side of his nose. "Top secret."

The door to the gym opened. It was PC White.

"Thank you, Mr Jefferson, I'll take over now."

Jefferson clicked his heels and saluted. "Permission to speak, sir."

PC White said to someone outside the door, "Could you take Mr Jefferson for a cup of tea, please?"

"That one," Jefferson nodded his head at Ryan, "spilling his guts out, sir."

"Jolly good," said PC White. "That'll be all."

Once the door closed behind Jefferson and whoever was making him a cup of tea, PC White turned and glared at us. For a moment he didn't say anything and we looked at the floor. It's funny how at times like that you start to notice really small details of things, like the patterns and small scratches and bits of old trodden-in bubblegum.

"You do know. . ." PC White flicked a doggy treat disgustedly off his uniform, "that you've wrecked the welcome concert and caused serious damage to school property?"

Luckily me and Boy Dave are quite good at handling things like this.

"We tried to stop them," said Boy Dave urgently, "but they were too quick for us."

"Didn't you see us jumping up and down, trying to stop them getting away?" I asked.

PC White held up a hand. "Don't make it worse for yourself, son," he said.

Twenty

My dad sometimes says that when you drop a brick it's best just to leave it there. I first heard him say this to Mum. She was talking to Mrs White (who, by the way, is PC White's mum) at the Women's Institute fête at the village hall. I should say at this point that this is a totally creepy event and is like getting the opportunity to buy jam and cakes made by witches.

Mum and Mrs White were standing by the stall with jars of preserved body parts from newts and frogs called pickles and chutneys. Mum said, "If I were you I'd steer clear of the quince jam."

Mrs White said, "Oh really?"

"Oh yes," said Mum. "We bought some last year and it was disgusting."

"Oh really?" said Mrs White again.

Well, I won't insult your intelligence by carrying on with the whole conversation, but obviously somewhere along the line Mum, who had been incredibly stupid for most of it, realized it was Mrs White who had made the quince jam and that she was ridiculously proud of it and was the only one who ever made it. So Mum started saying, "Quince . . . quince. . ." like those were her dying words. Then she said, "Oh! Did I say quince? I'm so sorry, it's me. It's been so . . . you know . . . what with the summer holidays and that . . . I meant mince! Mince for mince pies. Yes," she finished lamely, "it wasn't very nice."

She had most likely realized that actually Mrs White could have made any one of the witch's potions for sale. Meanwhile Dad, who had managed to eat five fairy cakes in the time, said, "Ange, sometimes when you drop a brick it's best just to leave it there."

I have been wondering if the grown-up way of getting out of things might be better. Boy Dave and I always start by telling lies straight away, but I think grown-ups have a special code, which means they have to pretend to believe what each other are saying, even if it's obviously nonsense and mostly complete gibberish.

Anyway, I thought of this all too late, and they banged on and on like old barn doors about the hole in the science-lab roof. Dad said the expense would ruin us and Mum said she'd never hold her head up high again and Joanna dabbed her eyes with a hanky (dunno what that was meant to be) and said I was, like, some kind of monster sent to torment her. I said we'd only been trying to protect the future of all humanity, but, obviously, as this had nothing to do with mince pies, no one cared.

Early on Sunday afternoon Boy Dave texted to say there was to be a meeting in the woods at the back of his house and could I sneak out when I was meant to be in my room.

When I got there Claire and Daisy were there too. They only want to know us when there's no youth club or older boys to hang with. I think they think we're a bit boring.

I tried to pretend I wasn't pleased to see Claire, so I said hello to Daisy and not her. Of all the girls I like Claire best. She talks quite normally and has long orangey hair. She's really clever as well and she always seems to be happy even when no one else is.

Yesterday had been crisp and autumny, but today the woods looked really green and the air was damp.

"We've decided to show them how serious it is and teach them a lesson," said Boy Dave as I sat down on a damp log.

"Mine seem to think it's pretty serious already," I said gloomily.

Claire and Daisy giggled.

"You misunderstand," said Ryan. "They must be made to see that the existence of aliens is proven fact and they ignore it at their peril."

"Crop circles," said Ryan. "You have to put bits of

rope through holes in the end of a board and then you lift the board up and trample it down in some corn and you keep on doing this until you've made an intricate and ornate pattern which only makes sense when viewed from the sky."

We nodded. We'd all heard of crop circles. Normally aliens make them with high-powered equipment from their spaceships. But we didn't really have time to wait for the aliens. At this rate we were going to be grounded until the end of the year. Then again, talking of trouble; "But what about the farmer?" I asked. "What about if he sets Blaze and Flame to guard the field?"

"They're sheep dogs," said Ryan, cross at being interrupted, "not guard dogs."

Claire said, "If we want it to look really proper someone will have to work out a diagram of what it should look like from the sky."

"What about a skull and crossbones?' suggested Boy Dave. "Then they'll be really scared and probably beg us to go back on the roof and try again."

"We were doing really well," I said thoughtfully. "They were practically going to land. It was only because. . ." I had been going to say that it was only because the lights had gone out, but then I had a horrible thought – what if it hadn't been that at all? What if they had sucked a piece of Nemesis's food up into the spaceship to analyse and got a really bad whiff of it? I tried to put the thought out of my head and hoped the others hadn't noticed me going red. I mean, surely the aliens wouldn't have taken it the wrong way; for all they knew, humans loved dog food and thought it was delicious.

Claire and Daisy looked at each other pityingly and whispered something about a helicopter. Then Daisy said, "I think the crop circle should be more like a symbol. Sort of something that would make sense to the aliens but not humans."

Claire said, "I could have a go at drawing up some designs on the computer if you like?"

"I reckon," Boy Dave was starting to look bored, "the best thing to do would be to just go down there and see what we come up with."

"Look," said Ryan sternly, "if we're going to do this we have to do it properly. Real crop circles are normally symmetrical. They have concentric or spiral patterns and sometimes small auxiliary circles and patterns as well."

I should say at this point that me and Boy Dave didn't have a clue what he was going on about.

Twenty-one

That night I pretended to go to bed early and sneaked out down to the field to meet the others. In the darkness, corn is a bit eerie actually. It stops being gold and is more of a sort of grey. A cold wind was blowing in off the hills and the corn moved in different directions as if a giant hand was brushing across it. Boy Dave and I stood at our end of the field shivering with Nemesis, who wasn't cold because of her fur, and was pretending to be a snake. We'd decided to start at opposite ends, with Claire and Daisy on the other side and Ryan "coordinating" (being lazy), and just make lots of circle patterns. We didn't really have time to think up a proper design and, to be honest, it was only a question of making a few patterns.

Boy Dave pulled at the rope. "It might be easier to pick up the board and carry it."

"I think we're meant to pull up on it and push the board down with our feet to squash the corn," I said doubtfully.

"I've got a better idea," Boy Dave said. "We can just drag it along and stamp on it afterwards."

As time went by our arms started to ache. Nemesis had disappeared into the middle of the field and the moon, which had started off bright, got hidden behind a big cloud. I began to get sick of the corn. It kept getting in our eyes and brushing against us. Some people think corn is really nice and go on about it being golden and yellow and summery and they go: "I must go into the corn for my picnic." Then it scratches away at their flesh until all that's left is bones.

By the time we had done our trampling and hidden the boards in the woods, it was almost midnight. Boy Dave's house is right at the bottom of the hills and not very far from the cornfield, so we said goodnight to him first. We watched him jump over the wall and run across his back garden. Then he let himself quietly into his house through the back door. We headed off down Hangman's Lane.

The branches meet overhead in Hangman's Lane and it was pitch-black. We live in a small village and there aren't any street lights so we all carry torches at night. The beams from the torches bobbed on the dry mud in front of us and baby rabbits kept getting stuck in them and staring at us from wide glowing eyes.

"How did your crop circles go?" I whispered to the others.

Claire said, "Why are you whispering?"

I shrugged, feeling a bit silly. "It just seems like the

sort of night where you should whisper." I looked into the darkness of the trees on either side and said in a scary voice, "You don't know who or what might be listening."

But Claire just said, "You're probably right. We don't want anyone to know it was us."

"We won't really have any idea of the sort of pattern we've created until daylight," said Ryan boringly.

I suddenly had a depressing thought. "How will we get away to find out? Me and Boy Dave are both grounded and it's Monday tomorrow; everyone will be up early."

It was OK for us to do things late at night, because we could pretend we were in bed asleep, but in the morning it would be really hard. Ryan's glasses glinted in the torchlight.

"We'll just have to get up before anyone else, and get back before they've woken."

"I'll never manage that," I said sadly. "I don't even have an alarm clock and if I did it would wake everyone."

"I know," said Claire, "you can sleep in my dad's shed. The key's in a pot by the door and it's got his sleeping bag in there for when he goes night fishing."

"Cool," I said coolly. I didn't want Claire to think I was a bit nervous of sleeping in her dad's shed on my own.

"And I'll climb the wall and bang on Boy Dave's window in the morning," said Daisy.

It didn't feel as if me and Nemesis had been asleep for ten minutes before Claire creaked open the shed door. Her jumper was inside out and she was still wearing her pyjama bottoms.

"It's time," she said grumpily.

Her dad's shed smells of damp and the floor is really hard. I sneezed and Nemesis gave Claire a snobby look and growled. I felt grumpy too.

Claire said, "Bless you," and started to laugh. "Your hair!"

"Your jumper!" I said rudely.

We felt in better moods after that.

Daisy had thrown a lump of mud through Boy Dave's open window to wake him and he still had dirt all over him when we all met up at the corner of Hangman's Lane. By this time it was five thirty. We had to hurry. Our dads get up at six thirty to go to work. They like to be out of the house by seven.

We raced up the chalk path to Crow's Ridge, then away across the field until we were standing right at the edge of the hill looking down. Beneath us our efforts of the night were spread before us.

Twenty-two

There was long, long silence, then Boy Dave said, "It sort of looks a bit like a face if you tip your head on one side. I mean you can just about make out an eye."

"I don't suppose there's any chance of getting all the corn standing up again before the farmer wakes up," said Daisy sadly.

Ryan considered for a moment. "One might be able to reverse the directional effects of the board, but I suspect the corn would simply fold over in the other direction."

"Don't worry," said Boy Dave bravely to Claire and Daisy, "we'll say it was just us."

"Maybe we aren't up high enough?" suggested Claire.

"When our dads see this," I said, "there will not *be* anywhere high up enough." I should say at this point that the corn looked like nothing on earth and definitely didn't have concentric or spiral patterns and small auxiliary circles.

It was about quarter past six when Nemesis and I got home.

"Maybe they won't know who did it?" Boy Dave had said on the way back. No chance. Through the back window I could see my mum and dad sitting at the kitchen table waiting. Slowly I put my key in the lock.

I'm not going to say much about that week. Many people moaned a lot. The farmer tried to get ASBOs on us and it seemed as if the whole village had divided itself up into two groups, which was the builders and all Big Dave's and my dad's lot, and then the farmer and Andy from the pub and the whole village hall committee, who decided that me and Boy Dave, all on our own, were spoiling the village and leading everyone astray, including Ryan (!!!). This always happens because Ryan's really good at school, and his mum, who is completely batty, forgets everything the day after it's happened. Our dads, on the other hand, tend to make a big thing of it and go round agreeing that we were in the wrong and are generally just totally disloyal, which encourages everyone to go on even more.

The only good thing to come out of it this time was that in the end our dads got fed up with it all and started saying it was only boys being boys, and my dad actually said quite a few serious swear words in the emergency village hall committee meeting. (Which they made him go to, and then changed their minds and made him leave.)

We had hoped it would all die down a bit so that we could just get on with our lives, but instead it was like a horror movie when just as you think *The Thing* has been killed and will never move again, its evil claw hand reaches out and it rises up. And this happens so many times that you end up just feeling a little bit surprised every time they kill it, and a bit less surprised every time it comes alive again, and not even at all surprised that it mauls someone else to death before being killed again.

That next Sunday evening Mum and Dad made me sit down at the kitchen table. They had serious faces.

"Jordan," said Dad, "I'm not going to raise my voice to you again." He was holding a piece of paper in his hand, "But there's something you're going to have to do."

I fidgeted. "I've already said I'm sorry about a zillion times."

Mum sighed and put her head in her hands.

"Sorry doesn't do it, son." Dad shook his head. "The damage to the school roof comes out at seven grand alone, and the farmer's field is more than that." He coughed. "As you know, we've been a man down on site and still had to pay him. Me and Big Dave are losing a hundred pounds a day in wages, plus having to do his job for him. That's five days' extra work a week, which we're having to do for nothing. We don't have the money to pay for the damage you've done. Simple as that."

I would rather he'd shouted at me instead of all that serious explaining. Mum sat quietly as Dad unfolded the bit of paper he was holding.

"What do you want me to do?" I asked. I had a lump in my throat.

Dad coughed then, as if he was going to say something he didn't really want to have to say. "The school have said that we don't need to pay for the damage to the roof as long as you and Boy Dave agree to take part properly in the reality television show. They've also said that, if it goes well, they'll pay for the damage to the field. But it all depends on this one thing, and you have got to – you hear me – *got to* do this right."

Twenty-three

Our school is always trying to make money. Mostly this is from jumble sales, where there are many things with monstrous patterns, and the stench of decay is everywhere; also school concerts and plays, which are pretty much the same. Mum said this is because our school is only part funded, which is something to do with it being small, and it has to pay for most things itself.

From what Dad said we were supposed to be cured by The Agnetha and then the damage would be paid for and the school could have even more money. Mum said the whole village was depending on us, even the village hall committee.

After that terrible serious talk with Dad, I went and sat in the garden. I needed to think. Of course I'd had to agree to let myself be cured by The Agnetha, and I supposed Boy Dave and Ryan had done the same, but, when I came to think of it, I wasn't really sure how to let myself be cured. I mean, I supposed we could do stuff like cuddle the little guys, but surely they didn't expect us to actually pretend to enjoy it. The only other option seemed to be to get genuinely brainwashed, and then I might never be the same again.

Normally I like the garden. It's a nice colourful place with bright flowers and raggedy crazy paving leading down to an old stone bench. Tonight, though, the shadows seemed whispery and eerie and the leaves moved as if someone was hiding in the bushes. At the sound of a voice beside me I almost jumped ten feet into the air, but it was only Dulcie. She lowered herself stiffly down next to me.

"'Just for a handful of silver he left us'," she said, looking at me wisely. Then she smiled. I like Dulcie's smile, it's calm and kind, but as if she's laughing at something inside; as if, because she's so old, she knows this big secret about life, which stops things mattering and makes them funny instead. She patted my hand, "There's a poem by Yeats, do you know it: 'Much did I rage when young. Being by the world oppressed'?"

I never know any of Dulcie's stuff, but she always pretends that I might do. I shook my head and she smiled again.

"Well, I thought you might like to know that you're not entirely alone. But the point is that we don't let ourselves be oppressed, do we, Jordan dear?" She stared off dreamily into the shadows. "And although we may don sheep's clothing we are never foolish enough to believe that this makes us into sheep."

As I lay awake that night feeling worried I thought about what she'd said. Dulcie has a confusing way of putting things, but sometimes I think this makes them mean more, like there's extra little meanings inside the big meaning. I stared into the darkness and I realized that at least she liked me the way I am, and that even though I had to go along with all the stupid things they wanted me to, I didn't have to become that stupid person. Actually, as it turned out, the sheep thing turned out to be important in more ways than one, but that wasn't until later.

It wasn't exactly sheep's clothing but the next day just before Monday study period, our whole class had to go up to Bobble. He clipped small microphones on to our shirts and put a battery pack with an aerial on the back of our trousers. We weren't allowed to take these off without permission. Last week there had only been one session with The Agnetha and we'd managed to avoid it. But there was no chance of avoiding them now.

Once we were all "miked up" we had to sit round in a circle on the floor.

"Now." (The Agnetha was sitting in the circle too.) "Does anyone know why we sit in a circle and not behind desks?"

Poppy Lockhart said, "So we can all see each other."

The Agnetha beamed. "Very good. And circles are kind, aren't they? It means we don't have any barriers between us."

Ryan coughed and pushed his glasses up his nose. "Interesting things, circles," he said. "You can't cut a piece out of a circle and shorten the distance of the original diameter on both sides."

"Mmm, yes," said The Agnetha, "now it's really important that in this group we accept people for what they are. That's the point of the circle: we are all equal in the circle."

Ryan coughed again. "Actually, I should think that true equality by positioning subjects in a circle would only really be possible in an endless void where the properties of all subjects or objects were identical."

The Agnetha said, "Thank you for your contribution to the group, David."

"Not only that," Ryan ploughed on, "but the properties of a circle are challenged by ideas emerging from the quantum theorists regarding wormholes and other ideas which challenge the accepted notions of order and continuum. In fact, the whole concept of time itself is quite subjective. I mean, while Shrodinger's cat was in the box there was no way of telling whether it was alive or dead and this supports the—"

"THANK YOU, DAVID," said The Agnetha, "I can see we're going to have to lay down a few ground rules."

Twenty-four

The ground rules were:

* We could only each talk for a minute (which meant Ryan)
* We had to respect each other's points of view (obviously ridiculous)
* We had to listen without interrupting
* We were only allowed to make positive criticism, and an example of this might be: instead of saying "I don't like the way you comb your hair" (like we all go round saying that all the time), you could say, "I think it would be really great if you combed your hair a different way."
* We had to try to be honest
* We had to support each other

After doing the ground rules on the white board, The Agnetha gave us all a bit of paper with the rewards we could earn written on it. Every time you managed to make an improvement on your behaviour you could earn a point. When you had managed to earn three points you could have a sticker for your sticker chart, and if you got ten stickers you would be able to join the school trip to Madame Tussaud's waxworks in London.

As we were walking home, Boy Dave looked at the bit of paper gloomily. "That's an awful lot of stickers to have to try and get."

Ryan said, "If you think about it, though, the teachers at school and your parents already think all your behaviours are negative, so there're lots of opportunities to change them."

"I wouldn't mind," said Boy Dave, "but it's not like I wake up every morning and say, 'oh good, another day. I think I'll go and do some negative behaviours'."

"Quite a lot of our accidents are because of your ideas as well," I told Ryan.

"Absolutely," Ryan agreed, "and I'm not saying we really should actually change or get brainwashed. What I mean is, you just have to work out what they want you to do and then they'll go, 'praise be, it's a miracle,' and give you a load of stickers."

Boy Dave looked at his rewards sheet again. "You'd think they'd have thought of a better school trip than having to walk round for a whole day going, 'Oh, look, another waxwork, doesn't it look real?'"

We nodded gloomily, but there was nothing we could do. We were stuck with it and there was no way out.

Twenty-five

In the Wednesday group meeting we had to be in teams of five. Me and Boy Dave weren't allowed to be on the same team because The Agnetha said that other members of the class might appreciate the chance to get to know us. I don't think this was really the case and Rhajni Singh actually had the cheek to say her mother wouldn't like it. I should say at this point that all the girls in our class are vile. Claire and Daisy go to Bellwood outside of the village, which is meant to be a posh school. Even so, they're the only two girls in the world who are actually a bit normal.

Obviously Poppy Lockhart was practically praying to be on Boy Dave's team because she wants him to ask her out. She'd have more chance of flying to the moon but she goes on sending Emma over to ask him and *yadeyadeya*.

The Agnetha read out the names for each team and it must have been Poppy Lockhart's lucky day because lo and behold she got . . . to be on my team instead. Ha ha! Boy Dave got Rahjni Singh and Lin Maize. Connor Keefe was on Ryan's team, which made him a bit nervous because Connor sometimes picks on Ryan because he's different and doesn't have fights or anything. I do think, though, that this doesn't actually mean anything about Ryan's potential for destructiveness. I should think the scientists who invented the atom bomb were probably not the sort who had fights either.

I'm not sure I would like to be Connor Keefe when Ryan becomes a famous criminal mastermind scientist and has a whole network of underground tunnels with little trains and foreign maniacs helping him to achieve complete world domination.

The teams were going to have names, which we had to think of as a group. Given that we were trying not to do negative behaviours I decided to be supportive.

"What about the Bullseyes?" someone suggested.

"Yeah," went everyone else, "that's quite good."

"I think it would be really good if we called it something different," I said supportively.

"I know," said Poppy, "what about Flower Power?"

"I think," I spluttered, "it would really good if we called it something different."

"The Camel Kids?"

What?

"I think it would be really good if we called it something different."

"AGNETHA!" they shouted. "Jordan is really spoiling it for the rest of us."

The Agnetha drifted over like a sort of weird mind-sucking goddess from *Star Trek*.

"I'm just saying," I said, "that I think it would be really good if we called the team something different from what they want to call it."

She smiled brightly. "Well? Have you asked Jordan what he thinks the team should be called?"

"No," they said grumpily.

"What do you think would be a good name for the team, Jordan?" she asked nicely.

I thought for a moment. "I think," I racked my brains desperately trying to think a sticker-earning sort of name, "well, probably the 'Say No to Mr Negative' team."

She beamed up at the silver camera. "Does anyone have anything to say?" she asked.

The rest of the team kept quiet. They knew a strike when they saw one. I looked modestly at the floor.

"We could call you the 'No Negs' for short, couldn't we?" said The Agnetha happily. "Right, everyone back in the circle."

Twenty-six

Once we were back in the circle the girls seemed to make an agreement to join forces. I don't know how girls manage to do this. It's like a wave of mind-controlling evil passes over them and they all start to think as one.

"Agnetha," Lin Maize put up her hand, "can I say something?"

"Of course," said The Agnetha, "the circle is a forum for sharing ideas."

"Well." Lin Maize has very perfect shiny black hair. When she stares at you her eyes are like little black circles of hate and she never looks away. "I think there are some members of this group who are only pretending to take it seriously."

I was a bit shocked to hear this. Up until this point I hadn't realized anyone was taking it seriously.

The Agnetha nodded slowly. "And how does that make you feel?"

Lin Maize looked surprised, but Poppy Lockhart waded in, "It makes us feel really angry."

"Yeah," went all the girls, "we're really trying hard, and they just want to earn stickers."

"Do these people have names?" asked The Agnetha sternly.

"David, Jordan, Ryan," they chanted evilly like some creepy religious sect.

Ryan seemed to take all this a bit personally.

"Actually," he stood up suddenly, "I think, of all the group, I'm the person who has taken the most interest and made the greatest contribution."

"Mmm?" went The Agnetha.

"Firstly," he continued, "I was concerned that the use of a circle didn't actually show proper equality, and pointed out—"

"Yes," said The Agnetha hastily, "I think we already covered that in the last session, David."

"HE'S NOT DAVID!" they shouted.

"He's Freak," sneered Connor.

"That's not a kind way to talk about your fellow student," said The Agnetha loudly.

"Also," Ryan continued, "I thought we were supposed to be earning stickers. I thought that was what you wanted us to do, and that the stickers were the reward for turning our behaviour around. Unfortunately, some of us have more behaviour to turn around, which means we have more opportunity to earn more stickers, but that is a fault in the system—"

"Thank you, Dav . . . whoever." The Agnetha looked nervously at the CCTV. When Ryan's on a roll it's pretty much impossible to stop him and The Agnetha was just finding this out.

"It's not our fault that some people like Boy Dave and Jordan have quite a lot of negative behaviours to change – LET ME FINISH!" Ryan yelled at the people who had opened their mouths to say something. "The level of achievement on reaching a target has to do with the effort required and. . ."

The Agnetha had gone a bit pink and her hair had started to fluff round the edges. She walked over and put her hand on Ryan's shoulder, "Jordan," she said bravely, "sit down for a moment."

"RYAN!" the class shouted and Connor said something rude. (I'm going to say no to Mr Negative here and not repeat it.) The Agnetha turned on him.

"NO," she said really loudly. She held her arm out like she was trying to stop traffic. "WE DO NOT USE LANGUAGE LIKE THAT! Go outside and sit on the stair for twelve minutes."

Connor looked at her as if she had gone mad. "What?"

"Go and sit on the stair," she said, hair fluffing wildly.

When I got home my mum said Connor's mum was going to go up to the school about this. Connor's mum thinks that on his way to school Connor skips happily, with daisies in his teeth, and pats the heads of small children. I don't think she sees Connor as the rest of the world sees him, which is stubby and mean with no neck, like a freckled robot. My mum said that once Connor got outside the classroom he got confused and didn't know which stair he was meant to sit on, so he went home. His mum said he was really upset because The Agnetha had made him feel stupid and destroyed all his confidence. When I pointed out that he is really stupid, Mum said, "Well, he might not be the sharpest tool in the box, but he doesn't need to be reminded."

I said nicely, "He's got to face it, Mum, or he'll never be able to turn his behaviour around."

She looked at me weirdly but Dulcie said it was certainly advantageous to know one's limitations and that the world would be a much better place if certain people had realized they were far too stupid to be the President of America.

At tea Dad was in a disgustingly good mood.

"They tried to teach you good behaviour yet?" he asked in a jolly voice.

"I think if we do what she wants we get some rewards or something," I told him.

Dulcie said, "Oh yes, bribes. In my day it was thought to make for spoiled and immoral children."

"No, Dulcie," said Mum, "this is different. They get rewarded for good behaviour."

"Yes, Angela," said Dulcie. "Bribes."

Dad said, "And this is all going on telly, is it?"

"Yeah," I said miserably, "I think we're going to have quite a big part in it, actually."

I didn't like the way Dad was smiling. "I expect you are, mate," he said happily.

Mum gave me a stern look. "Is there something you've forgotten to give me, Jordan?"

I made my eyes big and tried to look as if I was searching my brain. But then I saw the look on Dad's face and it was like his good mood suddenly evaporated.

But how could they know? Unless The Agnetha had actually phoned up my house to tell them. The thought of her talking to my mum made me feel really creepy inside. What had she told her? Had she tried to brainwash my mum as well? Maybe she already had. Not that they really needed much brainwashing, I thought gloomily as I went into the hall, where I had left my schoolbag. With a bad feeling I reached down to the bottom and took out a little bottle of pills.

The Agnetha had given one bottle of the pills each to me, Boy Dave and Ryan just before we left for home that evening. "These are wonderful," she had said.

It was the first time I had seen her do this particular smile. She reminded me of a fortune-teller who had just looked into a crystal ball and seen something bad, but had kind of enjoyed it. I think we made up our minds then and there to never ever give the pills to our mums.

Mum took the bottle and read the label. "Right, you're to have two a day after breakfast and tea."

Dulcie looked shocked. "Really! Nowadays a child only has to be naturally high-spirited and everyone labels him ABCD and pumps him full of drugs."

I got a scared feeling in the pit of my stomach. "Are they. . ." I whispered, "*mind-altering?*"

"Don't be ridiculous, Jordan." Mum glared at Dulcie. "They're omega three capsules: fish oils to help calm you down."

"Omega three?" I quavered. "Calm me d . . . down?" My hair was practically standing on end.

"Yes, Jordan. You may as well have one now."

Up until this moment I had secretly always thought that if anyone tried to do anything really bad to me my mum and dad would get angry and do something. I would have done anything to spit the capsule out, but Dad stood over me holding a glass of water until he knew I'd swallowed it.

The omega three capsules didn't just sound like something you'd launch off the *Voyager* to intercept enemy ships, they felt like it when you swallowed them as well.

"You've got nothing to worry about, son." Dad looked pityingly at Mum. "They won't work."

But for a whole hour after I'd taken the pill, I waited for something bad to happen. The way it seemed to me was like the television people had bought us – so they owned us. So The Agnetha could do anything she wanted and no one would try to stop her. What happened the next day at school just went to prove it.

Twenty-seven

When we got in to assembly we were surprised to see Shaggy with the long furry microphone and Bobble with a camera on his shoulder.

The Agnetha was standing at the front with the headmistress, who said, "Dr Barns would like to say a few words." She stood to the side and started clapping. There were a few other lame claps and The Agnetha came on as if she was the star celebrity on a chat show.

"Thank you!" Her teeth were dazzling. "There are two people in this room I'd like to come and join me here on the stage," she said dramatically, "Two young men who I, for one, am really proud of right now."

At this point I should say that me and Boy Dave were busy. We were right in the middle of a game of strings. We were using apple strings, which are the really bitter ones; eating them is like having your mouth sucked in by a million lemons. In this game you had to wind two apple strings round a bar of chocolate and put it all in your mouth at once. Once it's in, you're not allowed to touch it or spit any out.

"Jordan Smith and David Garret."

We suddenly realized that everyone was staring at us. We started chewing as fast as we could.

"Would you two boys please come and join me here on the stage." The Agnetha was clapping massively.

It was like being forced to be on *Jeremy Kyle*. We tried to pretend it wasn't us. We figured that if we sat tight for long enough everyone would move on to something else and forget about it, but the next thing we knew Jefferson was dragging us down to the stage by our collars.

By the time he had shoved us into the middle next to The Agnetha my strings felt like Mustaveajammydodger's tail dangling down the back of my throat. I think me and Boy Dave had almost choked to death on the way. We were about to wish we had.

The Agnetha didn't seem to notice. She put an arm round each of us. The cameraman came nearer and suddenly the microphone was hovering overhead. "Only a week ago," said The Agnetha, "these boys were in big trouble. Their negative behaviour had made them outcasts in their home town and their parents couldn't control them. They were on the verge of being expelled from school and their futures were truly bleak."

Even the headmistress looked a bit confused, but she just coughed and stared into space.

"Now," The Agnetha carried on triumphantly, "in just a week, with a little support and some controls and boundaries put in place, we have seen some truly great improvements." She beamed terrifyingly at us. "And have a guess who that's all down to."

We stared in panic at the sea of hate, which was the rest of our school.

"Go on," The Agnetha asked joyfully. "Who do you think has helped these boys turn their behaviour around?"

Someone threw a sandwich at the stage.

"Me?" asked The Agnetha grandly. "The school? The parents? NO," she cried. "Guess what? The people who have done this amazing thing are these two boys right here! Jordan and David. It's down to them. They decided to make the change all by themselves, and haven't they done well?" She started to clap happily and the teachers joined in pathetically but the noise of booing from the rest of the school was much louder.

Jefferson jumped to his feet. "Youse lot will shut your sorry mouths!" he yelled. "On receipt of command word clapands you will clap your sorry 'ands together. Even if it does make you sick to do so."

There was silence.

"Right," shouted Jefferson, "Troop, listen in. Troop, clapands!"

There was a tragic round of applause. The Agnetha's hair had started to fluff but she was determined to keep it all going.

"Is there anything you two boys would like to share about your experience so far?" she asked.

"No," we muttered.

"Oh, come on." She seemed to have recovered really quickly. It was as if all the other stuff had never happened. "Jordan, how about you?" It was like a nightmare. But we had to go along with it because otherwise our dads would kill us.

"I," I blurted out (the furry thing moved closer), "I think it would be really good if you combed your hair a different way."

We swerved the canteen at lunch to avoid being lynched for being total creeps, and went down to lie on the bank below the playing field. Gloomily we watched the sticklebacks swimming happily in the stream.

"This is torture," said Boy Dave at last. "At this rate we'll have to run away and join the Foreign Legion."

Ryan, who had been peering over the top of the bank, said, "I don't want to make it worse, but I think they're interviewing Joanna."

Twenty-eight

We lay down flat and peered cautiously over. Joanna was a little further along the edge of the field sitting on a bench with Collette. Beside her sat The Agnetha and in front of them was the film crew.

"Oh no." I put my face in my hands. "This is dire."

Quietly we scrambled along the edge of the stream to just below where they were sitting.

"So," The Agnetha was saying, "it's been kind of tough having Jordan as a brother, right?"

I could just about see the back of Joanna's head. She was nodding and Collette was stroking her arm comfortingly.

"Like," said Joanna tragically, "I guess we've never had it easy. But even when times were really hard we always looked out for each other, you know? But then he started running with the wrong crew. It's like no one can reach him now? Like he's a total stranger?"

I know Joanna wishes we lived in downtown Manhattan but this was ridiculous. I blame Collette. I think Collette goes home every night and practises how to talk gangsta rap. She gets some of it from CDs but she probably makes a load of it up as well.

Year ten all think Collette is really cool and obviously knows 50 Cent personally. To hear her banging on you'd think her mum sat round in a tiny apartment block dissing the police and going on about how life is really tough raising keeyads in the hood. I wouldn't mind, but her mum and dad won't even let her watch television unless it's "educational". She even has to come round ours to watch *Friends*.

The Agnetha said, "You blame the people he hangs out with?"

"Well, like, I know it must be his fault, too," said Joanna, "but when he was a little boy he was so cute, you know?"

Boy Dave and Ryan started to laugh. I should say at this point that Joanna has never ever in her life thought I was cute.

"It's been real tough accepting the way he's changed," she told The Agnetha, "and, like, I just can't believe the stuff he's mixed up in nowadays."

"What sort of thing is that?' asked The Agnetha gently.

Joanna's voice quivered, "Well, like, my Justin Timberlake lampshade, you know? I mean he just took it from my room."

"Ye-eas," said The Agnetha doubtfully, "and then there was the arson to the school?"

Joanna looked at her gormlessly.

"If," encouraged The Agnetha, "perhaps you said something like: you can't believe your own kid brother would make an arson attack on the school."

"Oh right," said Joanna lamely, "but, like, I think that was sort of an accident?"

"Or the vandalism when he destroyed the farmer's whole crop of wheat for the year?" said The Agnetha desperately.

I don't think she had realized how completely self-centred Joanna is and that, obviously, she couldn't care less about the science-lab roof or the farmer's "whole crop of wheat for the year" because these are things from the outside world, which, to Joanna, is mostly an inconvenient grey mist.

"Yeah," said Joanna, "but, like, he knew my lampshade was really special and he just took it anyway?"

Collette jabbed her finger in The Agnetha's face. "You hear what my girlfriend here saying, yeah?"

"Mmm," said The Agnetha disappointedly.

If The Agnetha didn't really like that interview much, she must have hated the next one. Just before we went in from lunch we noticed quite a lot of people gathered in the corner of the playground. The Crazy Frog Man was standing at the edge of the crowd and he seemed to be arguing with The Agnetha.

"You can't seriously let this madman go ahead with this?" she was saying.

"What, are you crazy?" he said enthusiastically. "This is great television!"

In the middle of the group was Jefferson. Shaggy and Bobble were circling round him with the camera and microphone, and he was looking very pleased with himself.

"National service!" He stuck his jaw out and rocked back on his heels, "Learned a boy discipline! Learned him respect and how to take care of hisself; keep 'is boots polished like glass and his shirt creased like razors and how to sit in nettles for a long time without complainin'. Boys in those days wasn't running riot with wishy-washy sticker reward load of rubbish. It would be DROP AND GIVE ME TWENTY AND THEN YOU WILL BE PICKING UP ALL THE TINY BITS OF DUST FROM THE OFFICERS' MESS WITH A PAIR OF LITTLE TWEEZERS! Yes," he said a bit more thoughtfully, "discipline and respect for a superior officer, providing they has come up through the ranks and is not some ponce what went to college."

The Crazy Frog Man pushed his way through the crowd. "So you don't agree with Dr Barns' methods?" he asked.

Jefferson stuck his hands behind his back and puffed up his chest. "In battle," he said, "you never

134

use your own field dressing on a wounded soldier. Lessons in life see? Proper lessons. Enemy bearing down at two o'clock, you don't tell him to go and sit on the stair, do you?"

"Em," said the Crazy Frog Man, "so you're going to show Dr Barns how it's really done?"

"Correct," said Jefferson. "I will be taking the new recruits into the woods. From then onwards they will be relying solely on their wits and training and anyone what fails in his duty will be scrubbing this yard with a toothbrush until it shines."

Beside me Miss Fairjoy, our form tutor said, "Oh dear." She tapped me on the shoulder. "I think you'd better go and fetch Miss Stormberry."

"Who?" I asked.

"The *headmistress*, Jordan!" she said crossly.

When I got to her office, the headmistress – whom I now knew was also Miss Stormberry – was sitting at her desk with a little piece of paper in one hand and a small glass of water in the other.

"Hello, ducky," she said. Her nose was looking a bit orange, "Jordan Smith, isn't it?"

I nodded. "Em, Miss Fairjoy says you'd better go to the playground straight away."

"Why?" Miss Stormberry sipped her water.

"Well, I think it's because Jefferson's doing a sort of interview."

"I know." She looked at the little bit of paper happily then she turned it round to show me, "Cheers." She raised her glass.

I peered at the paper. There were five zeros: five zero zero zero zero zero. "Five hundred thousand pounds," I said at last.

"Absolutely," said Miss Stormberry. "Very good. Top of the class. Well done, Mr Smith. Five hundred thousand pounds. Every penny of it going towards the school fund . . . naturally."

"Aren't you. . .?" I hesitated. "I think Miss Fairjoy wanted you to stop Jefferson."

"Stop him!" She looked at me as if I was insane. "They've just paid me half a million pounds not to stop him."

Twenty-nine

It was pointless me trying to pretend there was no letter home about the adventure camp with Jefferson. The dark forces in the village had probably already sent news by crow. That evening at tea I handed it over.

Mum read it quietly and her eyebrows slowly raised further and further up her forehead. When she was finished she passed it to Dad.

Dad reads really slowly, so we carried on eating. If you wait for him to finish reading something you end up in a sort of coma.

"I think I'll bring Nemesis to the village fête," said Dulcie casually.

Nemesis was sleeping on Dad's special television chair (which has a dent the exact shape of Dad's bottom) and didn't seem to realize how bad things were. Dad was reading, so he didn't hear.

Mum said, "I think we'll talk about this later."

"Don't," I asked, "any of you actually care that we have to go camping in the woods with a crazed maniac?"

"It's only for three days," said Mum unsympathetically, "and we won't have people chasing us for money any more."

Dulcie said, "In my young day it was all boy scouts. They used to go off for weeks on end."

"But not with Jefferson," I wailed.

I was starting to feel like the one who is the last to turn into an alien and who suddenly realizes he is surrounded by people who look like his family but who have really all been turned into aliens and that everyone he trusts turns out to be one.

"Oh, *Jefferson*," said Dulcie, "Always so. . ." she searched for the word.

"Homicidal?" I suggested.

"So . . . eager," said Dulcie finally.

I should say at this point that when it becomes completely impossible to understand anything Dulcie is saying it normally has something to do with Shakespeare, and that this use of the word *eager* was most likely something to do with him and must have meant something totally different from what I would take it to mean.

"At least Jefferson doesn't parade around in shorts and a little scarf and a woggle," said Dulcie, "And I doubt he'll make you all sing jolly songs round a campfire."

"No," I said sadly, "I don't suppose we'll be doing that."

Dad finally finished reading the letter and tried to guess what we'd been talking about. "Will you stop going on about that wretched animal!' he said. But he seemed in quite a good mood. He tapped the letter and raised his eyebrows at Mum. "Adventure camp, eh?" He actually grinned. Dad doesn't grin that often. It was a bit worrying. "Half a mil, eh?" He reached out and batted me across the back of my head. "It's not many kids who are worth half a mil. Hang on a minute," he fished for his mobile, "wait till Big Dave hears about this."

Moments later I could hear him in the hall talking to Big Dave.

"Yer, I know. Adventure camp. Ha ha ha." (That was him laughing.) "Jefferson, yer. Ha ha. We'll be getting them on *Big Brother* next ... yer, tropical island. But half a mil, mate! Yer ha ha ha." And so on.

He was putting his boots on for the pub. They obviously thought it was a night for some sort of celebration.

With a massive feeling of doom I got Nemesis's lead and took her for her walk down to the youth club. As I walked past the lighted windows of the Black Horse I could see my dad, Big Dave and a gang of other blokes all laughing and joking and raising their pint jugs and doing "cheers mate". Even Andy, the grumpy landlord, didn't look too miserable.

*

That night it was seniors' night at youth club. As me, Nemesis and Boy Dave walked up towards the lights of the Village Hall I suddenly realized that in another week it would be October. We'd only been back at school three weeks, but while all the chaos had been going on, the nights had been getting quietly darker and the last wisps of summer had drifted away. When I kicked the leaves at the side of the road they were crackly with frost.

Claire and Daisy would normally have been busy trying to get the older boys to take notice of them, but they were interested to hear the latest.

"So the television company have paid the school half a million to let Jefferson take you camping in the woods?" said Claire slowly.

"Not just us," Boy Dave told her. "The whole class."

We were sitting outside the village hall on a bench. Boy Dave and me still felt a bit uncomfortable around the rest of the school at the moment. Especially our class, who blamed us for having to go to the woods with Jefferson.

The nights were starting to get really dark now. Over near the trees in Hangman's Lane an owl hooted mournfully. It was like an omen.

The letter we had to take home said that Mr Jefferson was going to take the year eights on an adventure camping expedition for a week as part of the documentary and that the television crew had paid the handsome sum of five hundred thousand pounds towards the school fund. Any parents wishing their child to be exempt could write and ask for their child to be excused, but as the school was part funded and desperately needed money to stay open, and the new school gym would be a nice thing to have, and blah blah.

"What do you think he'll make you do?" asked Claire nervously.

"You never know with a madman," I said, trying not to sound worried. "It could be anything. On the other hand, if we weren't going into the woods with Jefferson, we'd have to do everything The Agnetha says, and some of her stuff is pretty terrible too."

Claire nodded thoughtfully. "I suppose, at least with her you don't have to stay the night. I don't want to be the one to say it, but you might be about to go out of the frying pan into the fire."

We spent the rest of the evening playing death or glory in the graveyard, which is a game Ryan made up and is a bit complicated to explain. But even when me and Boy Dave won three times in a row it still didn't take away the nasty thoughts I was having about the days to come.

Thirty

That Friday afternoon was the final circle meeting with The Agnetha before the weekend. She seemed to have gone back to giving us all love and understanding and it was hard to believe that we hadn't just imagined all that other bad stuff. I started to realize that it was only if you didn't go along with her that the other side started to come out.

"Now," she looked round meaningfully, "before I give the stickers out we're going to do some team building. And guess what?" she said, like there was going to be a big surprise. "This is going to FUN!"

Which was a surprise, and also turned out to be a bit like Dulcie's use of the word "eager".

We had to go down to the stream at the bottom of the playing field, where there was a plank of wood, four plastic bottles and a bit of string for each team.

"Now," explained The Agnetha, "the first team to make a raft and get one of their team across the stream wins this bar of chocolate."

She held up a huge bar of chocolate and Poppy

Lockhart said, "Ooh, yummy."

I should say at this point that Boy Dave, Ryan and me have got quite a lot of experience at building rafts. We've managed to make rafts out of some very unusual things. We even made a raft out of Ryan's mum's installation model thing and that floated very well in the end. But one thing was for sure: we were so definitely not going to be able make a raft out of the plank, the bottles and the string.

Later on Ryan did say rather a lot about volume, capacity and distribution of load, which was his way of saying the bottles were far too small. Still, The Agnetha was obviously very excited about them and the situation being what it was, we weren't about to burst her balloon.

My team all bent over the bits and fiddled about pathetically.

"I know," said Poppy Lockhart, "why don't we tie the plastic bottles to the plank?"

"Yeah!" said everyone else.

As if there were so many other things we could have done.

"Or," I said, "we could tie them to your hands and feet and lie you across the plank and you could paddle round and round really quickly!"

They considered this for a moment then Steven Longacre said, "I don't think that's very safe."

"And you could sit on her," I suggested.

"I don't want to have to get wet," said Poppy nervously.

I don't know how long we'd all been messing about tying bits of string on to the plastic bottles and planks. Anyway, after a bit our pointless efforts were interrupted by the sound of a whistle being blown. The Agnetha was standing at the edge of the water, clapping her hands enthusiastically.

"Ohh-kay," she said, "how have our teams done?"

We shambled down to the edge of the stream with our pathetic attempts. Obviously they were pretty much the same except for Ryan's team. I think he must have done a design of the one which would sink quickest, because the back two bottles were filled with water and the front two were on top of the raft.

"Excellent!" said The Agnetha as Shaggy and Bobble slithered about in the mud. "Now! The big moment! Who would like to go first?"

I put my hand up shyly. "It was Poppy's idea," I said. "I think she should be the one to get to go first and have most of the chocolate when we win."

The Agnetha beamed. "Thank you, Jordan, and what a nice example of team spirit." She did a mini round of applause.

"I don't want to have to get wet," said Poppy again.

"Actually," said Ryan, "I think it would be best if Connor went for our team. After all, it was his idea."

Connor looked confused.

"And," said Boy Dave, trying to outdo us, "I was really looking forward to it but. . ."

Lin Maize fell for it. She was in there like a speeding bullet. "I think it should be someone else," she said, giving him a snake stare.

Boy Dave shrugged. "But there's no one else who can make it, so it'll have to be me."

Lin Maize put her hand up. "I would like to be the one," she told The Agnetha.

"It's not my decision," said The Agnetha smugly. "This is something that must be worked out as a team."

Boy Dave decided to quit while he was ahead. "OK," he said sadly, "I think Lin should be the one, then."

Thirty-one

We did actually win the chocolate. I expect Ryan could explain this in a scientific way but basically it was because Poppy Lockhart is very round and probably a bit airy, like a balloon.

"I don't really want to. . ." she was saying as we cheered wildly and cried, "Lie flat on the plank, Poppy! Paddle round and round with your hands, Poppy."

"Don't worry," I said kindly, "I'll give you a good push off."

Meanwhile Connor sank like a stone.

I should say at this point that Lin Maize was spectacular. She lay out on the plank and paddled madly with her hands. When it started to sink she gave up paddling and clung to it as if she was trying to hold it above the water. When it turned completely over there was a moment where you couldn't see her but she must have jumped up from the bottom because, with a sudden mighty splash, she reappeared lying on top of the raft. And this happened seven or eight times and would have been more except The Agnetha waded in and dragged her out. I think the raft had probably moved about three centimetres.

Me, Boy Dave and Ryan did very well on the stickers that day. Poppy Lockhart, Lin Maize and Connor all had to go home early, and I heard Miss Stormberry saying something to The Agnetha about typhoid and pneumonia.

Poppy Lockhart got the chocolate, because she managed to get about halfway across, although, despite what, even I have to admit, was a stunning effort, she did actually get very wet.

As we were going home that afternoon The Agnetha was hanging round the lockers giving out leaflets. Her hair was particularly fluffy.

"Jordan!" she said brightly. "David!"

"Hello," we said politely.

"Would you do something for me?" She stared at us really meaningfully. "Would you read this carefully and try to remember what it says?"

I thought it was best to be honest. "We don't normally read handouts," I told her. "And we definitely don't remember what they say."

She looked over our shoulders. "Ryan! I was just giving Jordan and David these leaflets to read. . ."

"They don't normally read handouts," said Ryan, trying to walk quickly past.

"But I'll bet *you* do," said The Agnetha encouragingly. "Maybe you could help them to understand what it says. What it *really means*."

"It says to remember," Ryan took the leaflet and peered at it as if it was in a foreign language, "that you have rights and no one can make you do anything you don't want to do. You should remember that we are all individuals and just because someone is an adult they still don't have the right to push you about."

Me and Boy Dave started laughing.

"What it *really means*," he explained, "is that she doesn't want us to do what we're told on the Jefferson boot camp."

"We have to," I pointed out, "or they won't pay for the cornfield."

We'd been gradually edging towards the door and were at the top of the steps when a sudden cold wind blew bits of rubbish and leaves across the school yard. Unfortunately, The Agnetha had been edging out with us. She pointed to one of the classroom windows.

"If Mr Jefferson told you to jump out of there, would you do it?"

"Easy," said Boy Dave, "but we never get to do stuff like that, anyway."

"At the end of the day," pointed out Ryan, "once we're on Jefferson's camp, we're going to have to go along with it, the same as we have to humour you."

The Agnetha looked shocked. "Is that what you want? For people everywhere to think that marching kids round the woods is a great way to teach them positive behaviour and social skills?"

"Look," said Boy Dave impatiently, "all we *want* is to pay for the damage and get on with our lives."

More rubbish scudded across the playground, and as The Agnetha looked down at us from narrow, red eyes I had the idea that she was making the wind herself. I started to wonder if, underneath it all, she was just as cracked as Jefferson.

"So you boys think it's OK for my nurturing, caring methods to be seen to fail?" she asked coldly. "For my life's work to be made a mockery of? For some jumped-up, unqualified army misfit to try and trash my reputation?"

Normally Boy Dave gets angry first, but – I don't know if it was because I remembered what Dulcie had said, or because The Agnetha suddenly seemed to care a whole lot more about her own life than ours – I just felt as if I'd had enough. I folded my arms crossly.

"We're not sheep. And I don't think it's very caring to make films pretending we're worse than we really are."

Boy Dave and Ryan frowned warningly and The Agnetha looked at me oddly. Then she said in a really sickly-sweet voice, "No one's doing that. I know that

149

deep down you're good kids. It's just that, sometimes, showing how much we care can be a really hard thing to do."

"You told me to spray that can on the wall," I said. "It wasn't being vandals like you're going to make out. We don't even do spray cans."

"Yeah," said Boy Dave, "and making out we jumped on the desks in front of the teachers and that our class was shouting and swearing at Fern, when it was just your stupid role play."

The Agnetha's expression was starting to have an eerie effect on me. She should have been angry, but instead she gazed at us with a cold, dead stare.

"I suppose," said Ryan, "it's because until we did the thing with the roof and the cornfield you lot didn't really have much to make a programme about. And now you do, you want to be the one to cure us and not Jefferson, but that's just because you want to look good."

To our surprise she did a nasty little laugh.

"You know what?" The look she gave us was just like the one the older boys in the skate park give us when we try to get a go on the ramps. "You kids have got a lot to learn about life."

"What do you think she meant by that?" asked Boy Dave as we walked away down the steps.

"All we can do," I said sadly, "is just go along with her when we're with her, and with Jefferson when we're at camp. I mean, as long as the school gets its money I don't suppose it really matters."

Ryan frowned. "There's more to it than that. She doesn't want us to cooperate with Jefferson."

"Yeah," we said, "we do know."

"No, I mean, she *really* doesn't want us to. She won't just give in, you know." Ryan shook his head worriedly. "I don't trust her."

Thirty-two

Every September there is the village fête, held by the Women's Institute on the village green. That Sunday it was the fête and, as usual, everyone decided to go.

Dad and Big Dave normally go into the beer tent first and then come out and have a bit too many gos on the coconut shy. They are also normally a bit rude to the people who dress up in medieval costumes because the men have to wear tights. (I should say at this point that Ryan is dying to dress up in medieval costume, in the same way as he's dying to play the church organ, but so far no one's ever let him.)

Nemesis was wearing a check bow tie, which made her look quite well behaved, and she wiggled importantly down to the fête and was actually pretty good.

I'd arranged to meet the others by the hot-dog van, so as soon as we got there Dad and me peeled off. Nemesis decided to come with me. Obviously she thought it would be more exciting than sticking with Mum and Dulcie. Joanna and Collette were being serving wenches at the medieval feast table because

Adam from the butcher's was doing the whole pig on the roasting spit and they both want him to ask them out.

The air was cold that morning and had that brilliant smell of fried onions, which makes you feel hungry even if you're not. We sat on the grass and ate our hot dogs. Claire was wearing a green parka jacket with fur on the hood. She said, "Ryan says that psychologist woman wants you to mess up the adventure camp thing. You'd have to be careful," she wiped ketchup from her mouth on the back of her sleeve, "you might push Jefferson over the edge."

"Well, it's not just that." I gave Nemesis another bit of my hot dog. "I mean, we'll be stuck out camping with him. I suppose we could try not to do what we're told, but Jefferson will only think up dire punishments. Anyway," I added, "it's not exactly as if we don't do what we're told. That's the trouble; all our negative behaviours are accidents in the first place. I mean, take last time – we were just trying to protect the future of all humanity."

Daisy said, "I can't help thinking that if you just be yourselves it will all go wrong anyway. I mean," she said quickly, "just because you're so unlucky."

"Well, anyway," said Boy Dave, "it's different now. We don't have to do what she wants any more."

Thirty-three

The crowd seemed to part as if by magic, and there, by the medieval cheese stall, was The Agnetha. She was trying the cheese and chatting to two of the old crones from the Women's Institute while the film crew circled round. The Crazy Frog Man was there too, smoking a roll-up and talking to Bobble.

It was as if The Agnetha sensed we were there because she looked up suddenly.

"Great to see you guys," she said loudly, holding out her arms as if she was really pleased to see us. "I'm just enjoying some of your home-made country food. It's amazing. The people in this village are so talented!"

It was the first time Nemesis had met The Agnetha. I'd vaguely noticed her rocking about at my feet but I should've paid more attention because it was then that she did the same thing to The Agnetha as she did to Dad. The Agnetha, not being as steep as Dad, was obviously much easier to climb. One second she was going on about the wonderful cheese and the next, Nemesis had locked on to her neck like a vampire.

It was like someone had suddenly activated the Crazy Frog Man because he started jumping about going, "No . . . no . . . keep it rolling. Zoom in, zoom in."

"Grrummm," said Nemesis.

I looked round desperately. "We need some water."

For a bad moment I thought we were going to have to throw the great vat of medieval cheese over them, but then Boy Dave shoved a big silver jug into my hand, saying, "Here, use this!"

Without thinking I slung the contents at Nemesis and The Agnetha. A sudden strong smell of beer filled the air. Nemesis slithered to the ground and sat down, calmly licking herself.

"Sorry," I said quietly.

The Agnetha looked up and, just in time, saw the camera rolling right next to her face. She obviously said something totally different to what she had been going to.

"Well, accidents will happen." She sounded scarily calm. "I had a little dog myself once, but I'm afraid it used to get fur on the furniture." She gave the crones from the Women's Institute a horror-movie smile. "No matter what I did, the fur just kept coming. In the end I had to have him put to sleep. Such a shame." She looked down to where Nemesis was quietly licking her tail. "We'd better call the RSPCA. They'll do it humanely."

It took a moment for this to sink in. When I realized what she meant I couldn't believe it.

"But it was an accident," I said shakily. "It wasn't her fault she just . . . does it sometimes."

"I'm afraid that doesn't change anything," said The Agnetha sternly. Beery strands of hair were sticking to her face and her eyes had gone red. It made her crazy-looking. "That dog is vicious and out of control and will have to be destroyed."

Then it was as if something had suddenly occurred to her. Her eyes flicked open and she stared over our heads. After a while she said slowly, "I mean . . . it's all here on film. And there are witnesses." (The crones nodded enthusiastically.) "On the other hand. . ." her voice became suddenly kind-sounding, "perhaps I should think about it first – you know – own it a little – make sure I'm doing the right thing. After all. . ." It was as if her eyes were boring right though mine into the back of my head. "I wouldn't like anything to spoil our great working relationship. I mean – all the great progress you've been making with *me*."

At that moment the Crazy Frog Man absent-mindedly stubbed out his roll-up in the vat.

"Do you mind!" The crones turned on him. "That is prime-quality medieval cheese!"

"No kidding?" He stared into the vat. "That's incredible." He beckoned to Bobble. "Close as you can

156

on the six-hundred-year-old cheese. And the village people don't mind all that mould – no?"

"Herbs," said the crones. "The green bits are herbs."

We took the opportunity to slip back into the crowd.

Thirty-four

"It's lucky she changed her mind," I said, "about having Nemesis put down straight away."

It was about a quarter of an hour later and we were standing watching the morris dancers in the middle of the green. Opposite I could see my dad and Big Dave with their pint glasses like two big Teletubbies. It made me feel suddenly nervous.

Something else was making me nervous too: Claire, Daisy, Ryan and Boy Dave were all looking at me in a really weird way.

"What?" I asked crossly.

Boy Dave shook his head and did an annoying little laugh and Ryan pushed his glasses up his nose. Claire and Daisy looked uncomfortable.

"You don't understand, do you?" Claire put her hand on my arm. "The way she said it . . . 'the great progress you've been making with *me*'?"

"'With *me*'," I muttered to myself. For a moment I couldn't think what she meant. "OH!"

"Hallelujah!" said Boy Dave rudely.

"It was her way of saying," explained Ryan,

although, by now he didn't need to, "that if we manage to wreck Jefferson's camp she won't tell the police or the RSPCA about Nemesis attacking her, and Nemesis won't have to be put down."

"But it wasn't that bad." I started to get a desperate feeling inside. "Probably she's the only one who would take it seriously, anyway."

"They will take it seriously," said Claire. She looked tearful. "There's been lots of similar stories and they always destroy the dog. Always! No matter how much it isn't their fault or how much their owners really love them and try to save them."

Boy Dave patted me on the back. "It's all right," he said bravely, "we know she only attacks bad people – and your dad. We'll just wreck the camp like The Agnetha wants and no one will ever know."

Ryan frowned. "I still don't trust her. She won't do anything until after the camp, but it's very important that we get Nemesis to a place of safety before it's over. Once The Agnetha's got what she wants she might change her mind and show the film to the police."

"Maybe Nemesis is just really good at sensing when she's in danger," I said gloomily.

As it happened, it would probably have been better if Nemesis's sense of danger had actually lasted a bit longer.

*

It was about halfway through the morris dance that she shot out from under our legs and charged, tail flying, across where they were dancing, before disappearing back into the crowd.

Two of the morris men fell over but they weren't very badly hurt and managed to get up and find their sticks again. The one who had fallen and poked himself in the eye was helped to the corner, and the St John Ambulance people dabbed it with cotton wool from their pouches. I think a few people started to try and find Nemesis and there was an announcement over the loudspeakers about *could the person whose dog it is please keep it under control.* Opposite, my dad was drinking his pint and pretending that Nemesis was nothing to do with him.

Bravely the morris men carried on. Everyone started to clap and a few people really enjoyed it and carried on clapping in time to the music.

I whispered to the others, "We've got to do something. If she keeps on doing this sort of stuff everyone will believe The Agnetha."

Boy Dave twisted his mouth. "I don't think there's anything we can do. She's probably gone a bit weird from licking off all that beer. Oh no. . ." He nodded towards the crowd, where a small brown creature was crawling stealthily through people's legs, "it looks as if she's going to try for another pass."

Seconds later, Nemesis on turbocharge hurtled towards the dancing again.

This time some people tried to chase her, but she was faster than a speeding bullet. The morris men tried to dance out of her way, but instead of running for cover, which she most likely would have done if she hadn't had the beer, Nemesis began to chase them round and round. Confucius, who had been watching with Mrs White, obviously couldn't stand being left out any more. Barking at the top of her voice, she broke free and, with her lead still dragging, rushed over and joined in.

By now there were normal people mixed in with the morris men and the dogs. The jolly music was still going but no one was dancing; instead they were doing rugby tackles, trying to catch Nemesis and Confucius. The St John Ambulance people were standing by with a stretcher.

I should say at this point that I don't think it was bad enough for a stretcher, but normally they just get to do a few wasp stings and sit someone down who's had a funny turn, so you can't really blame them for getting excited.

Somewhere along the line Confucius and Nemesis, who seemed to have made friends, realized they'd better quit while they were ahead and rushed off across the field. Nemesis had one of the sock bells in her mouth and also the strap and also some bits of sock. The last thing we saw or heard of them was jingling as they disappeared into the woods.

Thirty-five

After that everyone tried to carry on and enjoy the fête as best they could. Tinky Winky and Laa-Laa (our dads) had a go on the coconut shy, which surprised everyone (not), and also had a medieval feast. Mum took Dulcie home because Mrs White was going round blaming Dulcie and Nemesis for everything.

That lunch time everyone was gloomy. Dad wasn't home because he'd gone off with Big Dave, and Nemesis was nowhere to be seen.

"We have to find her before it gets dark," said Joanna. "Poor little Nemesis will be so scared."

Dulcie said, "Well, really, all that jangling and jingling and bashing about! What do they expect? There was absolutely no warning. And that dreadful Confucius creature—"

"But where could she have gone?" interrupted Joanna tearfully. "She should have come home by now. Maybe she's lost and can't find her way back."

Mum put her hand on Joanna's arm. "Don't fret, love, dogs are very good at finding their way about."

I coughed. "Me and Boy Dave will go and look for

Nemesis if you like. We could go and look in the woods."

"You would, like, actually do that?" Joanna looked at me weirdly.

"Course," I said, "anything to help out."

I didn't dare tell them about what had happened. If Dulcie and Joanna found out that Nemesis might be put down they would be heartbroken. Also, with PC White being Mrs White's son and, given all the fuss Mrs White was making about it all being Nemesis' fault, I figured the police might be out looking for her already.

"Oh my God," Joanna turned to Mum, "it's really working. He's really changed." She put her hand on her chest and opened her eyes wide. "I'm going to have a really cute little kid brother!"

I tried not to choke on a roast potato.

"Hey," said Joanna excitedly, "you could come into Brighton with me and Collette and we could, like, get you some really nice clothes? And we could buy you an ice cream?"

"No thank you," I said politely. "I'd rather stand on my head in a twenty-foot cow pat."

Joanna looked a bit upset. Mum said, "Jordan! She was trying to be nice."

I glared at them. "I said I'd look for Nemesis, didn't I? I didn't know she would start all that. And I haven't changed. You're all making out as if you hated me before."

Mum patted my arm. "We all love you, Jordan, and we always have, it's just. . ."

Joanna said, "Actually, I did hate you. And also – my Justin Timberlake lampshade? I just want you to know that I'll never, ever get over it."

Straight after lunch we met up in Boy Dave's den. It used to be the garage, but his dad's done it out with a floor and heating, so it's brilliant in there. There's some old chairs and all Boy Dave's stuff, even a little fridge with drinks.

"All this thing with Nemesis," I said after a while, "it would be terrible if she really did have to go – you know – like Mustaveadonut had to go."

Boy Dave looked shocked. "She hasn't actually eaten anyone, has she?"

"Well, not as far as we know, unless she's eaten Confucius, but I think they're actually friends. Having said that, we thought Mustaveadonut and Mustaveajammydodger were friends until it happened."

"Trouble is," Boy Dave went over to the little fridge and got out some cans of fizzy orange. He threw one over to each of us, "tonight's the last chance to get her back. After that it's adventure camp."

We sat and drank our fizzy orange and it was as if a black cloud was in the garage, hanging right over our heads.

"If we can get the dogs back," said Ryan in his scientific voice, "we could hide them in a safe house. That way this thing with Jefferson and The Agnetha won't be so much of a problem. I think a good start might be to try and find a smell that they are particularly attracted to and trail it along the ground into some sort of a trap."

"Is there a smell that lunatics are particularly attracted to?" I asked.

Ryan coughed. "Actually, I meant the dogs. Of course," he held up a little bit of paper importantly, "we won't really be wanting to dig a deep hole ourselves, so we'll use one that we've found – like a ditch or something."

We peered at the drawing. It showed a sort of side view of a hole dug into the ground, with lines, which were meant to be twigs, over the top. It was the sort of trap you see in old superhero cartoons where someone falls into it and the baddies stand looking over the top going: *Ah-ha, not so easy to escape this time!*

"Right," I copied what Ryan always says, "small problem. It might be weeks before Nemesis and Confucius go that way and fall in."

"Two things," said Ryan. "Firstly, as well as tempting things like meat, dogs also really like the smell of aniseed and they can hear high noises, which we humans can't hear. We'll buy a dog whistle and stand near the trap, then we'll blow it really loudly – well, loudly for dogs – and Nemesis and Confucius will come rushing over. They'll smell the aniseed trail, which leads to the trap. Then they'll smell the tempting things and try to get them and fall in." He paused. "Now all we need is somewhere for them to fall into."

"What about the old air raid shelter on the other side of the woods?" suggested Claire.

"We could put the leaves and twigs over the top," I said, "and put some tempting things inside?"

"It's quite deep," said Ryan. "We'd need something soft for the dogs to land on, and we'd have to block up the doorway."

"There's a load of hay outside the horses' barn on the other side of Crow's Ridge," suggested Daisy.

"That's settled," said Boy Dave briskly. "We'll borrow a boat and get it tonight."

Thirty-six

The darkness seemed to come down fast that evening. By the time I reached the stables the sky was a silky-looking Halloween black and the air was filled with the trick or treat smell of burning leaves. The moon was only half full and it came and went behind ribbons of cloud, but no one dared switch on a torch.

The others were busy sliding the first hay bale down the bank towards the dark shape of a boat at the water's edge. At the top of the bank, the back end of the stables loomed creepily and we could hear the horses snuffling and stamping about inside. A couple of small bats flickered out from under the roof and roller-coasted down over the water. Claire must have been feeling the same Halloweeny feeling as me because she said, "This would be a good night for telling ghost stories round a campfire."

"I've never understood why people tell ghost stories," said Ryan in a boring voice. "If I wanted to frighten someone I wouldn't bother with ghost stories. I'd dress up and creep up on them. But before that I'd make lots of noises, like a werewolf devouring its prey and the sound of shuffling like something heavy being dragged. I might scream and whimper and say, 'Please spare me,' and then some more shuffling and devouring and a hideous scream, which would echo around and around like someone in agony. Then a low spluttering, gurgling sound and the drumming of heels on the ground and. . ."

"I think," said Daisy tiredly, "the idea is not to frighten everyone so much that they actually want to go home."

"There's no point in only half frightening someone," said Ryan crossly.

Luckily we were busy for the next few minutes getting the hay into the boat. Daisy held one end and I held the other while Boy Dave, Ryan and Claire tipped the bale in.

We had just finished the second bale when we heard the sound of an engine. To our horror we saw a set of car headlights were sweeping across the field towards us.

Thirty-seven

"Quick," whispered Boy Dave.

There was nothing for it. It was too dangerous to go back by the path now. We scrambled down the bank and into the boat. Ryan plonked in beside me at the front with Daisy and Claire behind and Boy Dave right on the edge at the back.

I grabbed an oar and started to row frantically, only to realize we were going round in circles.

"Get rowing!" I elbowed Ryan hard in the ribcage. "Or we are totally dead."

"Small point," the hiss came back, "I don't know how."

I realized then, that whenever we went boating, Ryan was always too busy collecting specimens to take a turn at the oars. He'd probably never rowed a boat in his life.

Up at the stables, the headlights – which had got brighter and brighter as the car drew nearer – lurched suddenly to a standstill. The engine stopped and there was the sound of a car door opening and slamming shut.

The next thing I knew Ryan was sprawled on the floor of the boat, and Claire, who had shoved him, was sitting beside me. She dragged his oar out of his hand. "Come on!" she said urgently. "Row."

I shouldn't have been surprised to find out that Claire could row – she can do most things.

Our oars made a quiet splashing sound as we dipped and pulled through the dark water, quickly gathering speed. We were almost starting to breathe again when Boy Dave, who had been crouching quietly at the back of the boat, suddenly hissed, "He's coming."

Claire said to me, "If we can just make it to that bend in the river we can pull in under the willow tree."

We fell silent, glancing nervously over our shoulders as the torchlight bobbed down the bank and started to swerve up and down across the water, searching. The dogs, Blaze and Flame, had followed the farmer down. It was so quiet we could hear them snuffling and panting as they sniffed the grass at the water's edge. They had found our scent, but with any luck the water was confusing them.

"What's that, girls?" the farmer was saying. "What you got?"

By way of answer the dogs started to jump excitedly, their dark figures flicking in and out of the torchlight.

I'd been so busy worrying about the farmer that a quiet hiss from Claire made me jump: *Slow down.*

She pointed to where the leaves of the willow were dangling like a shadowy curtain only a few feet away.

We glided through them into a quiet, leafy, little cave. We could still see the farmer's torch shining faintly through the leaves, but the branches went low into the water and with any luck they would be thick enough to hide us.

"Do you think we should carry on?" whispered Boy Dave after a few moments, when me and Claire had caught our breath.

Claire shook her head. "Too risky. We'd be out in the open and it'd take another few minutes until we were out of sight round the bend."

"What if we row through to the other side?" suggested Ryan. "We might be able to keep going with the willow between us and the farmer."

Claire looked at me. I shrugged.

"OK," she whispered, "but we'll have to be careful of reeds and branches near the edge."

Quietly we glided through the other side of the willow and carried on along beside the bank, using its branches as a shield until finally we were round the next bend and safely out of sight.

Not long after that the stream started to widen along the edge of the wood.

The woods are different at night. The trees seemed taller overhead, and dark. I was glad that no one was telling ghost stories right now, and that Ryan wasn't somewhere in the darkness making devouring noises. Still, the splish-splash of the oars and the fuzzy moonlight on the water helped to calm my nerves, and it wasn't long before we reached the air raid shelter.

We shifted the bales out, then Claire took the boat and moored it up, hidden underneath another willow.

Away from the water the night became pitch-dark. The only light was from Claire and Daisy's torches on the path ahead and it took all five of us to get each hay bale up to the air raid shelter and roll it down the slope where the steps used to be.

Ryan pulled the strings taut and Boy Dave cut them with his penknife. They did this all the way round, then we all picked up great armfuls and piled it up inside. When we had finished it seemed as if there was much more than when it was packed up tightly in bales.

"That should be all right," said Ryan confidently. "Nemesis and Confucius will have a nice soft landing."

We were shivering a bit by now and I think we were all feeling pretty creepy. The trees were creaking and rustling in the darkness and we could hear little animals and what might have been members of the Women's Institute scurrying about.

"Did you get the tempting things?" I asked the girls.

They pulled disgusted faces and Daisy said, "They're not really very tempting."

They went down to the boat and came back a few moments later with a heavy-looking carrier bag, which was filled with a lot of smaller bags. If you held one up you could see blood and gunk slopping about inside.

"The butcher called it offal," explained Claire. "He said we should probably cook it first but apparently it will definitely attract dogs."

"Vampires more like," said Boy Dave disgustedly.

But we didn't have much choice. I should say at this point that standing in the dark woods scattering blood-soaked bits of meat on to a pile of hay is probably something that only members of the Women's Institute would enjoy – and probably only on special occasions, like before the vegetable show.

It was starting to get really cold and trails of mist had begun to drift across the path like ghosts. I'll tell you something about the woods: you can play in them all day and be quite happy, but there's a time when you know you have to go. It's when a chill sets in and the leaves rustle loudly in the shadows of the trees. I think we all knew it was that time. As fast as we could we blocked up the door with a jumble of wood and stones and covered the top of the trap with thin sticks, reeds and bits of grass. Then, thankfully, we turned and headed for home.

We were halfway down the path when Boy Dave said, "What about the boat?"

We stopped and stared at each other in the torchlight.

"I don't think we should take it back past the farm tonight," said Daisy, "and we were meant to be home ages ago."

Ryan didn't seem too worried. "It's pretty well hidden."

"Don't you think you should take it back?" asked Claire, "I mean, not now, later on."

"No," said Boy Dave firmly, "we've always wanted a boat. And now we've got one it seems pointless to spoil it."

We got quite excited then. It would be great not to have to keep going up to the Black Horse every time we wanted to go boating.

But it was going to be a while before we did anything nice or fun again. The next day was D-day, or the first day of Doom Camp as it later came to be known.

Thirty-eight

To our dismay The Agnetha was waiting for us at the school gates.

"I wanted to wish you all luck," she said. "The very best of luck. Now," she put her hand on my shoulder; it smelled of a sickly sort of perfume and felt really heavy, "you won't forget what we discussed, will you?"

I looked at the ground and shook my head.

"And how is that bad little dog?" She laughed. "It's a shame it isn't human. We could do some work around its vicious behaviour."

"We'll do what you want and wreck the camp, OK?" said Boy Dave. "But don't expect us to pretend that we like you, because we don't."

"That's great," said The Agnetha. "So we learn to express anger. And we learn something from this, don't we? *You guys* learn something. You learn that my methods are the right ones." Finally she let go of my shoulder. "Don't let me down," she said suddenly. Then she walked away.

"Don't worry," said Ryan as we trudged miserably to assembly, "I'm working on a plan."

You should have seen Jefferson. He was dressed like an action man – full army combats with a little green beret tipped to one side. It looked as if he'd been trying to grow a moustache over the weekend. He marched out in front of the assembly with a bit of stick under his arm. The camera and furry microphone moved in.

The headmistress was sitting with a sort of fixed smile on her face, and The Agnetha boggled as if she couldn't believe her eyes. Beside me Boy Dave said, "Oh God," and covered his eyes with his hand.

Jefferson clicked his heels together.

"Right," he said loudly, "listen in. There are some sorry members of this school what need a lesson in discipline. What are year eight, what will be coming to the woods for adventure camp. YEAR EIGHT," he bellowed. "On receipt of command word 'stand up' you will be standing up. On receipt of command word 'walk on' you will walk on until you is all standing in front of me. Is that clear?"

We were too shocked to do anything.

"IS THAT CLEAR?" he yelled.

Some pathetic members of my class whispered, "Yes."

And that included Callum Mockford and Connor, who I have to say, looked a bit sick.

"YES, SERGEANT MAJOR!" shouted Jefferson.

"Yes, sergeant major," they whispered.

"RIGHT," yelled Jefferson, "YEAR EIGHT, STAND UP."

Ryan shocked us by suddenly jumping to his feet. "YES, SERGEANT MAJOR!" he yelled.

The whole school turned and looked, especially The Agnetha, who glared daggers.

We filed embarrassedly down to stand at the front. Out of the corner of my eye I could see Joanna. You'd think she'd have been enjoying it, but she looked quite upset and Collette had her arm around her comfortingly. I realized that Joanna was still pretending I was her little kid brother who liked being bought ice creams.

Jefferson's eyes were bulging. He walked along the line, staring at each one of us in turn.

"You have to be exactly like him," Ryan whispered.

He was standing in an unnatural sort of way with his chest puffed out like a pigeon and his hands behind his back.

Boy Dave whispered, "Humour him, yeah?"

"You, boy," Jefferson came so close to Boy Dave's face that their noses were almost touching, "shut it. Or you will drop and give me twenty."

Already some of the girls and Steven Longacre looked like they were going to cry and Connor's face was a sickly shade of green.

"YES, SERGEANT MAJOR," shouted Boy Dave right back in Jefferson's face. "Sorry, sergeant major."

Jefferson looked as if he was going to die of pride. "Better," he said as he strutted off, pigeon-style. "And you can stop your blubbing," he told Rhajni Singh.

"My," she sniffed, "my mother wouldn't like it."

Jefferson looked as if he was about to yell, but Miss Stormberry said in a stern voice, "Mr Jefferson, a word in your ear."

Jefferson clicked his heels and went over for his "word". I noticed the Crazy Frog Man then. He was standing at the back of the assembly hall and he seemed to be almost jumping for joy.

Thirty-nine

The morning didn't get any saner as it wore on. Jogging in Jefferson language is called "at the double", and we all had to go "at the double" to the woods with our stuff. What made it worse was the film crew crawled along beside us in a car, filming our agony. Also, quite a few people from the village came out to nudge each other and pull sad faces and shake their heads.

Jefferson trotted along with his stick, obviously not feeling at all embarrassed, which is strange, considering he looked so completely stupid. But by now he thought he was a soldier in *Full Metal Jacket* and had lost all contact with reality.

"We all do what we've been told?" he sang loudly in a questioning sort of way, which Joanna would have admired.

"We all do what we've been told!" sang me, Boy Dave and Ryan heartily while the others puffed miserably along and stared at us from gloomy, wondering eyes.

It's not far to the woods from school – probably

seven minutes or so – but it was a lifetime of humiliation.

Jefferson must have got up first thing in the morning to get everything ready. When we got to the woods there were little piles laid out ready on the ground. They had a silver tray, tin mug and some repulsive-looking tinned stuff. Also a green bit of plastic, some boot polish and a few other things – I never did find out what they were. Jefferson told us we was all to stand by our kit (which I think was the little piles), then he held up two bits of green plastic.

"These here," he told us, "is your cover for the night. You will be bedding down with one or two others."

He did a demonstration of how to put the green plastic up between two trees with some elastic things but we didn't take much notice.

"We have to do everything just as he wants," said Ryan later, as we were trying to fix the green plastic things to a tree. "If we can get him to trust us, we can start to get things back to how we want. I've been thinking," he added, "about showing you're in command."

"I don't know if Jefferson's exactly in command," I said. "It's more like everyone humours him because he's a lunatic."

"Exactly," said Ryan casually, "and we have to pretend we're just like him."

"Easy for you," muttered Boy Dave.

We put our green sheets up roughly for the moment and stood with our hands behind our backs and our chests out. Jefferson seemed pleased about this and told us we could "stand easy". I was going to leave it at that but Ryan had other plans.

"Sar'n't major," he said loudly, "permission to speak."

Jefferson twirled an imaginary moustache. "Permission granted."

"We would like to make ourselves useful, sar'n't major."

I should say at this point that Ryan has a lot of information in his head, which is normally only useful about once. I have no idea why Ryan had suddenly started to say sergeant as "sar'n't", except that I think they say things in a funny way in the army and Ryan seemed to know this. Actually, he probably knows quite a lot of stuff which will never come in useful and might even be a bit disturbing. He was being a bit disturbing now.

"Is there any extra jobs you would like us to partake in, sar'n't major?" asked Ryan. "To show we is not lazy."

Shaggy and Bobble circled excitedly round us filming everything.

"Very well," said Jefferson happily. "You will be gathering up some sticks – what will include big sticks and little twig sticks – what will be used for the fire."

"Yes, sar'n't major!" said Ryan.

We crept off into the woods.

"What did you do that for?" demanded Boy Dave. "Now we have to go round getting sticks."

"Well, first of all," Ryan slid down with his back to a tree, "we can escape for a while and plan the best way to mess it all up."

"Not for long," I said gloomily. "Shaggy and Bobble are coming to film us gathering sticks." They were treading carefully through the trees, trying not to get their wires caught in the branches.

We ran for it.

Forty

After a little rest hiding behind the air raid shelter (which, what with the hay and the tempting things was getting a bit smelly) we gathered a few twigs and headed back.

"We'll just have to say we didn't have much luck," said Boy Dave.

We needn't have worried. Jefferson had made everyone else gather sticks anyway and now he was trying to get them to make a fire.

"You put the big stick bits," he was saying loudly, "then you do put the little twig bits underneath and all around. And then you do set fire to them."

We sneaked into the group, making out we'd been there all the time. Meanwhile Jefferson began drawing in the dirt with his stick.

"Right," he said. "Listen up!" He drew an imaginary line down the middle of us, "You on this side will be Alpha Troop. And you," he poked his stick at everyone on the other side, "will be Charlie Troop."

Me, Ryan and Boy Dave were actually in the same

troop – Charlie – but Ryan slid across the line to the Alpha side near the front. Boy Dave and me copied him and also stood at the front, puffing out our chests. Boy Dave even tried twirling an imaginary moustache.

"You, boy," Jefferson said to Ryan. "Name?"

"Marconi," said Ryan loudly. "Private."

"Well, you is now corporal," Jefferson told him, "and you is in charge of Alpha Troop. And you is not to take any lip. And the rest of you pathetic lot," he said nastily, "will do what Corp Macaroni tells you, understand?"

"Yes," they muttered crossly.

Ryan turned round and glared at them. "The sar'n't major didn't hear you," he yelled. "What you meant to say is 'YES, SAR'N'T MAJOR'."

"Yes, s'blh mumble," said his troop pathetically.

Jefferson gave a nod and made his way over to our side. I must admit that I tried not to be quite as puffed out as Boy Dave and tried to stand a little bit behind him. And so it came to pass that Boy Dave was made Corporal Garret in command of Charlie Troop.

There were some instructions after that and the next thing I knew was Alpha Troop and Charlie Troop were both meant to be going in opposite directions.

Just before we split off Ryan marched his troop

alongside and said, "You get the aniseed and I'll get the dog whistle."

Poppy Lockhart was probably the only one who was glad to have Boy Dave as her corporal. She and Emma came and tried to talk to us.

"So," said Poppy cheerfully, "we have to go around the outside of the wood and circle back in again to see if we can take Alpha Troop by surprise."

Boy Dave looked at her as if she was from another planet. "Eh?"

"You know, and then assume positions and take our line of fire." She smiled and tried to take his arm.

Boy Dave dodged her. "Well, we have to get some aniseed first."

Connor, who had recovered a bit from his fear, started to look mean. "What d'you mean aniseed?"

"Don't you want to go to the sweetshop, then?" asked Boy Dave. "Or would you just like to walk round the woods all day and assume positions?"

I should say at this point that Connor is the greediest person I know. Most other bullies steal your schoolbag to throw it somewhere inconvenient like the top of the bus stop. Connor does it so he can check for food. Point being, as soon as the sweetshop was mentioned Connor didn't give us any more grief. In fact he trotted along quite happily.

A few more of Charlie Troop did try to say we

should be following the instructions and blah blah, but, as Boy Dave pointed out, he was the corporal and everyone had to do what he said and, also, he'd forgotten the instructions anyway.

By the time we got back to the camp we'd all had a few sweets and felt better. When Jefferson saw us coming he casually dropped his cigarette into the dirt and tried to stand on it so as no one would notice. He also hid his magazine under the log he'd been sitting on. (We had a quick look, but it was called *Camping and Hiking in the Cotswolds*, and was pretty boring.) He coughed loudly and said we was all to lie on our stomachs at the edge of the wood, watching the village green. This went on for a very long time.

After about two hours (when almost everyone had had to do a wee in the bushes), we saw Alpha Troop trudging tiredly in from the left.

Jefferson stood up and said loudly, "It would appear the enemy 'ave taken a wrong turn." And made us all turn round the other way so we could "fire" on them.

It rained heavily that night.

We probably noticed this more than the others because we must have made a mistake building the green tent. Normally a tent has a roof that slopes down on the outside so all the rain can roll off, but, for some reason ours had gone the opposite way and turned into a V shape. Where the two bits of green plastic were meant to overlap, rain was pouring through like a waterfall. As my ears filled up with water and my teeth chattered I started to wonder if I would freeze to death before I drowned or whether anyone had ever drowned and frozen to death at exactly the same time.

Forty-one

Before that night, I had never actually spent much time lying in a big puddle. The green things were deliberately designed to be very low to the ground so you couldn't sit up in them. Jefferson had explained that this was "so as to deceive the enemy" and that we was "not allowed to so much as move a muscle" for the same reason (apparently). All of which might have been quite useful if we'd been fighting in Afghanistan. But then again, in Afghanistan we most likely wouldn't have got all that rain.

"I think if the water gets any higher I'm going to drown," I told Ryan and Boy Dave.

"You are in the middle," agreed Boy Dave, "so you will probably be the first to drown, but we won't be far behind you."

"Thanks," I said, "that's comforting."

Ryan coughed wheezily. "We can't stay here or we'll catch cold."

Which was like saying, if we go into that plague-infested village with crosses on the doors, and cartloads of bodies, it might make us a bit sneezy.

"Do you think Jefferson would notice if we went home?" I tried to roll up on my elbow before the water completely filled my ears.

"We can't," hissed Boy Dave. "They'll kill us. The school will have to give the money back and we'll be in even more trouble."

"It could be part of the programme?" I suggested. "About how we didn't stay at the camp and actually went home to sleep in our beds instead?"

"No," Ryan gazed thoughtfully at the waterfall, "but if we sneaked really quietly out in the darkness we could maybe get to somewhere better than this."

Nervously we rolled over on our stomachs and peeped out.

The night around us was pitch-black. Just past the campfire we could see the film crew's van. The two back doors were open and a blaze of light shone out. The last time we saw Jefferson he had wrapped himself up in his green thing like a sort of hooded cape and was sitting by the pathetic campfire on guard. Now we could see him happily drinking cans in the back of the van and chatting and laughing with Shaggy and Bobble.

Right beside the van was the film crew's tent. It was like a little house. It must have been the shape of it that gave me the brainwave.

"Claire's dad's shed!" I said suddenly. "Where I stayed for the crop circles. They keep the key on the ledge above the door. And there's a sleeping bag there as well."

Ryan pushed his glasses up his nose.

"Right," he said in an active-sounding voice, "we're going to need clean, dry clothes and some sleeping bags and blankets. I'll distract them with a few devouring noises and you two raid the tent. I'll meet you back at Claire's dad's shed as soon as I can."

Forty-two

Claire's dad's shed wasn't the most comfortable of places to spend the night, but compared with the green thing it was great. The film crew's sleeping bags – which we'd borrowed – were nice and fluffy, and their chocolate biscuits were the sort that your mum only buys if someone's coming round, and you're not allowed to have one.

Their clothes were quite cosy too. Boy Dave chose Shaggy's big blue jumper, I had a red T-shirt and Bobble's bobbly cardie, and for Ryan we managed to find a green check shirt and body warmer which had been folded up neatly at the end on one of the sleeping bags ready for morning. While we were in the camera crew's tent we also made an important discovery. Me and Boy Dave don't like maths and normally only bother when it's to do with money, but even we worked out that if there are two members of a film crew they don't need three beds.

We stood for a moment over the nice cosy camp bed. It had a little pillow and a flask all ready for morning. Silently Boy Dave reached down and picked up the magazine that was lying there: *Camping and Hiking in the Cotswolds*! He held it up with a sickened look on his face. Jefferson!

So Jefferson was going to sleep in the cosy tent and let us all get rained on and drowned.

It hadn't been easy rushing off through the woods while the film crew and Jefferson bobbed torches about looking for the devouring creature. I heard Jefferson say something about sending up a shumuli (whatever that is), but luckily I don't think he had one. We didn't fancy actually sleeping in Jefferson's sleeping bag but we took it anyway, to put underneath ours.

Looking back we probably should have made a better plan than the one we did make, but we were a bit tired and wet and by the time we actually got our heads down we were practically asleep already. The next thing we knew, it was daylight and no one knew what time it was or even where we were for a bit.

The Agnetha wanted us to wreck the adventure camp, which, on its own, would have been quite easy. But it's actually quite difficult to *secretly* wreck an event. It requires cunning, skill and careful planning. We did realize that planning what to do in the morning, in the morning, wasn't really very cunning or skilful or careful but, in the end, I don't think fate had left us any choice.

I was telling Dulcie about it afterwards and she cheered me up a bit. She said that working out what to do in the morning, in the morning, had been quite popular with some recent important historical figures and no doubt I was standing shoulder to shoulder with my allies, which, of course, excused everything. I think she must have meant Ryan and Boy Dave.

I can't say our clothes had exactly dried out in the night but they were a bit less wet and we couldn't go back to camp wearing the Shaggy jumper, the bobbly cardigan and the body warmer because there was a chance the film crew might recognize them. I did wonder if our parents would sue the school if we all died of flu, but I expect the Crazy Frog Man would most likely give the school some money and everyone would agree he could make a TV programme about it.

The adventure camp was supposed to last for two more nights, but I think we'd already decided that, whatever else happened, we were going to spend those two nights at home in our own comfy beds.

By the time we got back to the woods, everyone else was up (since four thirty that morning, we later found out). They were all sitting miserably round in a circle polishing their trainers with boot polish. Jefferson – looking very grumpy, I have to say – was stomping about shouting that everyone should be able to see their ugly faces in their shoes by the time they had finished, and that foot rot was the worst enemy a soldier could have, and sand would wear your feet to the bone in the desert, and a lot of other information which wasn't really going to come in very handy.

We watched from a distance through the trees then Ryan said, "We'd better get a few twigs and pretend we thought we had to gather sticks again."

"Mmm," I screwed up my eyes trying to see, "I don't know if that's going to do it. He's looking especially barmy at the moment."

Boy Dave leaned back against a tree and said in a dramatic voice, "I'm just so tired of it all."

We nodded. We were tired of it all too.

"We have to go back," said Ryan firmly, "we're the stars of the whole show. Well, you especially," he added.

"Can't we just ruin it quickly?" I asked. "There has to be something that would do it."

Our class were sitting silently, polishing away, with barely the energy to lift their heads. By this time I think they'd lost the will to live.

"We can't end up like that," I said sorrowfully.

"No-oo," agreed Ryan slowly.

"It's the damp." Boy Dave coughed pitifully.

We'd had to change back into our own clothes, and they were starting to smell. And, he was right; the damp was terrible. It was like being wrapped in slugs.

"Well," said Ryan thoughtfully, "I think the best thing is to try and work out what would make good television. I mean – if we can wreck the camp in such a way that the Crazy Frog Man will like it, I don't suppose anything else matters."

"Er, small point," I normally enjoy using Ryan's expressions back at him, but this time I wished I didn't have to, "Jefferson might not like it."

"There is that," said Ryan thoughtfully. "On the other hand, if we make out it isn't our fault I don't see how he can do anything really bad to us. I mean, if we get Nemesis and Confucius back we can say we found some poor dogs trapped in the air raid shelter and stayed up all night trying to free them. And we can explain that we saw some of the evil gang members who trapped the dogs and that it's probably not safe to be in the woods and we'd all better go straight home."

I must admit I had a few doubts about this, but Boy Dave really perked up. "Yeah," he said enthusiastically, "and we could make our faces all dirty and tear our clothes and maybe make some small scratches for a bit of blood."

"A bit of blood always shows you've made an effort," agreed Ryan.

"Hold on a minute." I held up my hand. "If The Agnetha recognizes Nemesis she could still have her put down."

"I thought of that," said Ryan. "Firstly there will be two dogs, and she won't know which one it was.

Secondly, it'll be what the Crazy Frog Man calls great television. They're hardly going to go and ruin it by killing off the stars of the show, are they?"

"We can make it like a real film." Finally I was beginning to see a light at the end of the tunnel. "We can hold the dogs in our arms and say, 'well, little fella, you certainly had us all worried.'"

Boy Dave looked at me oddly. "I think it has to be a child if you say that."

"Yes, well," interrupted Ryan, "small point. . ."

Whatever his small point was going to be we never got to hear it. At that moment there was a rustling back along the path and the sound of muffled voices coming nearer.

Forty-three

"It's The Agnetha," I whispered. We were lying flat on our stomachs, behind a fallen tree.

"I want it on record," The Agnetha was sounding stressed, "that I think this whole boot-camp idea is irresponsible and abusive."

"It's legitimate methodology." This was the Crazy Frog Man. "Another approach, that's all – touchy-feely versus hard line. Tough love, that sort of thing."

"This isn't tough love!" The Agnetha said crossly. "You know nothing about tough love!"

They were coming into view round the bend in the path. The Agnetha was wearing a giant brown coat with what looked like bear's ears on the hood. Crazy Frog Man was saying, "Don't forget, we're paying you a big fat fee. This bloke Jefferson does what he does for the love of it. I call that commitment."

Boy Dave, Ryan and me looked at each other. Jefferson was doing the boot camp because he didn't see anything wrong with it. The fact that he really enjoyed it, and was obviously thrilled at finally being allowed to do one, was worrying, sad and slightly scary. At this point I should say that I haven't got a clue what "legitimate methodology" is but I didn't like the sound of it.

We stayed flat behind the log until they'd passed by.

"They'll be wondering where we are," said Boy Dave nervously. "As soon as The Agnetha gets there, she'll see we're gone."

We decided the best thing to do was to get on with Operation Rescue Dogs and fast.

We dropped the aniseed balls so they made a trail to the air raid shelter and sprinkled some on the false roof. Then we got out the dog whistle. It was obvious no one had fallen through the trap, so Nemesis and Confucius were still at large.

Through the trees we could hear the sounds of moving about and see shadowy figures. Jefferson was shouting, "TROOP, FALL IN, SINGLE FILE, WHILE THE CO DOES ADDRESS YOU."

We had a bad feeling.

"Quick," said Boy Dave, "get some dirt on your faces and scratch your arms a bit."

We hid behind the trees and scratched up with some twigs and rubbed mud on ourselves. Boy Dave was trying to rip his T-shirt up.

"I need scissors," he said crossly.

"Just take it off," I told him. "If we have blood and

no T-shirts it'll look like we've been really making an effort."

As soon as we looked bad enough to have been up all night dog-rescuing we stood on the furthest side of the air raid shelter and blew the whistle.

The next bit is confusing.

Forty-four

Firstly, nothing happened at all except that Jefferson's "troop" spread out in all directions and wandered miserably about in the trees. We slid down further and waited.

"Blow the whistle again," said Boy Dave in a low voice.

Humans can't hear dog whistles because they're too high, which makes it hard to believe they actually work.

Some members of the troop were getting close. When I peeked round the side of the wall I could see Cal Mockford and Connor trudging through the trees. By the looks of them they hadn't made their green thing properly either. In desperation Ryan blew the whistle again.

This time there were noises in the undergrowth. At first we thought it was rabbits but after a few moments we could make out a blurry shape coming through the trees.

"Maybe it's Nemesis and Confucius," I said hopefully.

"I hope the tempting things are still there," said Boy Dave.

The shape was coming straight towards us and, behind that, another one. Ryan shook his head. "Too big."

"Wrong animal," said Boy Dave. "They're sheep."

There were rather a lot of them actually. As we watched, more and more dirty, white, woolly sheep with staring eyes came trotting (quite quickly, I have to say) towards us. Ryan turned the dog whistle over in his hand and said, "Hmmn, that's interesting."

We'd forgotten about Jefferson's troop, but now something happened to remind us.

"What you doing?" demanded a thick sort of voice above our heads. Connor was standing dangerously on the wall of the air raid shelter at the edge of the trap. "Jefferson's looking for youse lot, and Dr Agnetha and that other bloke, and the television crew."

"Shut up," I told him. "We're busy."

"What you doing?" he asked again, jumping down on to the grass bank. "I'm going to tell them you're here." He was smiling an especially moronic smile. "And then you'll be in trouble."

"Aw," said Boy Dave, "that's clever. Did you work that out all by yourself?"

What with trying to keep an eye on the sheep and Connor we'd forgotten Cal Mockford, but suddenly he made us all jump.

"LOOK OUT!" he yelled in a high-pitched voice.

And it was weird because at that moment he disappeared underneath a sort of blanket of dog.

The dogs weren't Nemesis and Confucius, but it explained the sheep. I don't think anyone in the village has ever tried to say that Blaze and Flame aren't good dogs – they win prizes for being good sheep dogs. And this was proof.

As soon as they heard the whistle they must have been desperate to run to it but, being good dogs, they felt they had to bring the sheep with them. The sheep went quite still once they saw Blaze and Flame. They clumped together in a group, watching calmly.

Connor went green and said, "Uhh blub dog gurumm," and then, a bit more easy to understand, "DO SOMETHING!"

Ryan went down on all fours and tried to get a glimpse of Cal. "I don't *think* they're eating him," he said reassuringly.

"TROOP, FALL IN." Jefferson's voice sounded too close for comfort. "ON RECEIPT OF COMMAND WORD SHOOSHEEP, YOU WILL SHOO THE SHEEP. ON RECEIPT. . ."

We peered nervously around the edge of the bank. We could see some of our class making a few droopy shooing movements with their arms. Following behind them were Shaggy and Bobble (minus their jumpers), trotting over the undergrowth, looking almost enthusiastic. I could imagine what it would be like: a sort of documentary action bit where you know the person with the camera is running over bumpy ground. Behind them the Crazy Frog Man was doing a little dance like a pixie. But running faster than any of them was a giant brown bear. It was screaming at the top of its voice, "THIS HAS GOT TO STOP!"

Forty-five

What happened next was unfortunate. One minute there was a bear and then there was a horrendous crash. Perhaps everything might have been quiet for a bit after that. It's hard to say. But I think we did realize – even before a voice from inside the air raid shelter went, (Scream!) "OH MY GOD. SOMEONE HELP ME." (Scream) "THERE'S BEEN A MASSACRE" – that:

1 We had managed to wreck the adventure camp, and
2. That it hadn't gone very well

Boy Dave, Ryan and me tried to look inside the door to the pile of hay. It was The Agnetha. She was going, "Help, help," as she tried to climb up the wall. "Oh my God!" (Shriek) "Help me. Someone help me." (Gibberish bit) "Something terrible . . . unspeakable. . ." By the looks of it she'd landed right on top of the tempting things.

Ryan moved some of the wood and said, "You'd better come out this way. You're probably too triangular to climb out on your own."

By this time the Crazy Frog Man and Jefferson had both reached the top of the air raid shelter and were looking down into it with most of our class. I think they were past caring. They gazed listlessly at the crazed Agnetha and the tempting things. All apart from Lin Maize, who blinked her stony black eyes and said, "But this is disgusting."

I have to say at this point that Jefferson was about the most normal I have ever seen him, and that the Crazy Frog Man was scary. He danced on the edge of the wall yelling, "Wow! Quick! Get this. Film this. Quick."

Jefferson said, "But these is entrails what is as yet unidentified. Troop," he said quite normally, "you will go back to the camp and sit down and wait."

They turned and traipsed back, while Shaggy and Bobble tried to make it up the bank. Meanwhile the sheep had started to wander about casually, and Blaze and Flame had gone to look down at The Agnetha and the tempting things. Suddenly they too disappeared into the air raid shelter. At least someone found the tempting things tempting.

The Agnetha, who was, by now, trapped down there with two big (and probably quite fur-shedding) dogs, who were devouring the rather smelly tempting things, decided enough was enough. She headed for the door like an angry bull. Bravely she yanked the last bit of wood away and started to climb over the hay bale. Then she saw us. "AGGHHHH," she shrieked.

Rather surprisingly, she calmed down quite quickly. She looked at us with eyes like the sad, crazed, old man who tries to warn strangers away from the vampire castle.

"What happened?" she asked wonderingly. "Did someone make you do this? Did they make you take part in a ritual?"

At that moment the Crazy frog Man saw us as well. He yelled, "It's them! Pan to the boys. Get the boys."

Jefferson said, "Youse three! Get your sorry behinds over 'ere now."

There was only one thing for it. I decided to do what a grown-up would do. "Quince," I said. "Did I say quince? I'm so sorry – it's me – what with the summer holidays and that. I meant *mince*. . ."

"Shut up, you idiot." Boy Dave grabbed my arm. "Run for it."

But up ahead the farmer was calling Blaze and Flame through the trees. "Come by, girl! Come by!"

"Quick," said Boy Dave, "the boat!"

And we bolted for the stream.

Forty-six

There wasn't much time. Jefferson, the Crazy Frog Man and Shaggy and Bobble came charging after us. Luckily the boat was still tied beneath the willow where we had left it the night we set up the tempting things. We ducked under the dangling leaves and threw ourselves in. Quick as a flash Boy Dave slipped the rope and we began rowing for our lives.

For a moment they must have wondered where we'd gone but then Jefferson shouted, "Enemy at one o'clock."

And they all started charging along the riverbank.

"Head for the open sea," cried Ryan.

Shaggy and Bobble, with all the equipment, were getting left behind and the Crazy Frog Man was beckoning to them like he was bowling a ball and shouting, "Hurry up. Come on. Stay on them."

By this time he thought he was a top war reporter, although in reality he was just skipping along the path. I'd never seen anyone who couldn't actually run before. It's unfortunate in so much as no matter what dreadful thing happens – quick, it's the tsunami – and everyone will be running away, and then along comes Crazy Frog Man, skipping desperately. He can skip sideways too, which is a bit better I think, and slightly faster.

Up ahead we could see the fork where the stream joins the river, and the second bridge, which crosses from the edge of the woods to big houses with gardens right down to the water's edge. We rowed with all our might.

As the boat glided underneath the bridge it was like entering another world. It was eerie, echoing, and the water dripped from the brown walls – the sort of place where rats and trolls live.

"I'm knackered," said Boy Dave tragically. His face had gone bright red. "We'll never make it,"

"My arms are killing me," I agreed.

We looked at Ryan, hoping for ideas, but he was leaning off the edge of the boat, peering ahead along the river. From the darkness of the tunnel the water glittered brightly.

"There's something up there," he said, "on the mud."

As we got further under the bridge we could see it too: a small shape, down beneath the garden of one of the houses. Boy Dave half closed his eyes, squinting into the light. "It couldn't be Nemesis, could it?" he asked.

Now I came to think of it the little thing was a bit

like Nemesis. It looked like an otter, small and low to the ground, but something about the way it moved its head was familiar. We rowed towards it.

The creature was on the other side of the bank from Jefferson and the Crazy Frog Man. When it saw us, it came slithering down towards the water, yapping loudly.

"It's not Nemesis," I said gloomily. "Nemesis can't bark; she can only go, mmm, mmmm, mmm, like that."

"Well, it can't be Confucius," said Ryan, "because Confucius is beige."

Boy Dave and I gave him an odd look. I suppose beige is an actual colour but I thought only grown-ups said "beige" and normally only about furniture.

We rowed slowly to the bank where the creature was. On the other side of the stream Jefferson was shouting about futility and surrender, but the small creature started running about frantically and yapping even louder, drowning him out.

"It is Confucius!" I said excitedly. "She's covered in mud."

But Boy Dave and Ryan had gone quiet.

After a bit Boy Dave coughed. It was one of those coughs he hardly ever does and it's for when he's being serious. The last time he coughed like that was when he had to tell me his dad wasn't taking us to the football.

"What's the matter?" I asked.

The boat was drifting in now and it was time for us to get out, but Boy Dave and Ryan were sitting completely still.

Eventually Ryan turned round and pushed his glasses up his nose. "I'm afraid there's something else on the bank," he said in a grown-up voice, "and I'm sorry to have to tell you that it might be Nemesis."

"Well, that's brilliant!"

But even as the words came out of my mouth I realized it wasn't brilliant at all and I felt my face freeze over.

The riverbank is dark-brown mud, thick like clay. When the tide is really high, it disappears completely. There are stones in the mud and some clumps of dirty rushes and grass, sometimes even a dead seagull. As I turned to look I could see a furry jumper, which someone had thrown away – like it had been washed up on the edge and got covered in mud. Well, I tried to make it look like a jumper. I wished it was a jumper. But we were near enough now to see her head. And her ears. And the long crazy tail matted straight out behind her like a piece of old rope.

Silently we drifted in. Ryan and I stepped out and Boy Dave pulled the boat up the mud.

Forty-seven

Ryan was the first to go to her. Confucius was jumping up and down at his legs. She must have been waiting with Nemesis, and was really glad someone had come. Ryan knelt down next to the little muddy shape, which was lying quite still, and lifted her ear. Then he put his hand underneath her head and raised it up.

"She's caught in some fishing twine," he said, "it's all round her front legs. It leads back into the water – probably stuck on some weeds down there." He stopped. Then, in a quiet voice, he said, "She would have been trapped when the tide came in."

I thought of Nemesis charging round happily on the roof, that night of the aliens. And then I thought of her being tangled in fishing twine for hours with no one to rescue her. My eyes filled with tears. I brushed them away with the back of my hand but more came. Boy Dave coughed again. Ryan said, "You'd better give me the penknife."

It must have been only a few minutes while Ryan cut through the twine and shook Nemesis's paws free but it seemed like a long time. It was like I was there on the riverbank but I was somewhere else as well. And the rest of the world was fuzzy and cold, as if I was stuck all alone in the middle of ice.

Bravely Ryan picked up the muddy little body and held it to his chest. He was covered in mud himself now. It smeared his glasses; his jeans were thick with it.

Boy Dave picked up Confucius, who licked his face madly and tried to smother him with wriggling. He said, "Eeyuk." And dropped her into the boat. Then he got in beside her and picked up an oar. "We've got no choice now."

He looked over to where Jefferson and the film crew were standing watching. It was as if they knew, because no one was shouting any more.

Ryan tried to give Nemesis to me to hold but I shook my head and nodded towards the oars. I had to row.

This next bit is something I don't think I'll ever forget. Even when Ryan's being really boring and annoying I do remember this – he could have put Nemesis down on the floor of the boat but he didn't. He kept her on his knee with his arm round her, even though she was muddy and floppy and it wouldn't have made any difference to her at all. I suppose he did it because he knew it made a difference to me.

It was only a few minutes before we hit the mud on

213

the other side. Slowly me and Boy Dave stood up. Boy Dave got hold of Confucius and dropped her down, where she spiralled happily round and round before rushing up to the Crazy Frog Man and trying to wipe her mud off on his jeans.

Jefferson, who seemed to be getting more and more normal, walked down to the boat and helped us drag it up the bank. He didn't say a word and it ended up with us all standing together and him looking down at Nemesis. In the end he said, "I see you've taken casualties." He held out his arms and, for some reason, it seemed right for him to take her.

For a minute he held Nemesis, looking down thoughtfully. Then he lifted her eyelid, then the other eyelid. He turned her on her back and put his hand on her chest. Then he did the weirdest thing. He started to run.

We stared after him, not sure what to do, but at the top of the bank he turned round, "Dog needs a vet," he shouted impatiently.

"She's dead," I said back and my voice came out quavering and tearful.

"She will be," shouted Jefferson over his shoulder.

Boy Dave pushed me hard in the middle of the back. "Come on! Move!"

Forty-eight

Even though Jefferson's the PE teacher we'd only ever seen him run when we were running away from him, and then we normally had a head start. In lessons he just stands there going, "On receipt of command word ONE you will touch the ground," etc. as we go round and round. But he was fast. I don't think I've ever known a grown-up run so fast.

We managed to catch him on the path. Way back in the trees following us were Shaggy and Bobble, the Crazy Frog Man and Confucius, who liked the Crazy Frog Man's skipping.

Jefferson hurtled over tree trunks and clumps of grass, cuddling Nemesis to his chest. When we reached the edge of the woods he swerved away from Hangman's Lane and across the village green to the main road. We hacked it after him, turning left again and charging down the main street towards the vet's.

Jefferson kicked open the door. It banged loudly on the wall behind. The woman at the desk looked at us like we were bank robbers, but he didn't seem to

215

notice. He shoved past all the other animals and their owners and put his face close to hers.

"Vet," he said. "Now! Or this dog will die."

I blinked. I would probably have started crying again if I hadn't been so out of breath. Boy Dave hung his hand off my shoulder and Ryan folded his arms and looked at the floor. A few moments later a tall man with bright yellow hair came through and said, "This the one?" He took Nemesis and turned her over. Then without a word he headed for his room.

By the time everyone else arrived Nemesis had a little plastic bag hanging beside her just like on *Casualty*, and a silver foil blanket. One of the nurses was giving her a "bit of a clean up".

The Crazy Frog Man burst in, along with his new mate, Confucius, and said, "Right, fill me in."

The vet and the nurse stared. Ryan said, "It's all right, it's reality TV."

"Oh," said the vet, "right." Then he went a bit weird and started going, "Oh-kay so . . . what we have here . . . some lesions on the paws where the twine was wrapped around, you see? She was badly dehydrated and suffering from cold and exhaustion . . . probably had to hold her head up above the water when the tide came in . . . saline solution . . . blah blah . . . light sedative . . . blah blah . . . incubator. . ."

"Is this your dog?" Crazy Frog Man turned to me suddenly.

"It's my Aunt Dulcie's dog," I said. "She's called Nemesis."

"Can they make him better?" asked Crazy Frog Man.

The vet tried to say some more stuff but the Crazy Frog Man kept looking at me. "She was dead," I said. "Then Jefferson said she might be alive but if we didn't get her to a vet she would definitely be dead. Now. . ." my voice wobbled.

When Mum saw this bit on television she cried and said, "Oh, my little Jordie."

She would have liked it to carry on but luckily Boy Dave saved me from total humiliation. "Now," he said to Crazy Frog Man, "you can shut your stupid face."

We left Nemesis in a plastic tank. It had a light in it to keep her warm. She was still sleeping but she looked cleaner and comfortable and I was allowed to put my hand in and stroke her. Confucius had had a bit of a clean up as well and some food and water and the vet had checked her out. He said she was in "pretty good shape".

As we left Shaggy said, "Er, mumble, I couldmnmm a burger."

(We finally realized that this is how television crews talk because mostly they have to be quiet, so their mouths get saggy.)

"Mmm, yerrum some fries," said Bobble.

"You lads," said Crazy Frog Man to us, "fancy a burger, yeah?"

Suddenly we realized we were starving.

Forty-nine

The nearest place to get a burger and fries is Brighton. We were allowed in the back of the van, but Confucius wasn't because of all the equipment. She sat in the front with Jefferson and the Crazy Frog Man. It was brilliant. Shaggy and Bobble showed us (by using mumbles and hand signals) how to make a film of each other and play it back.

Unfortunately Ryan spoiled it a bit by making us interview him as if he was a famous scientist. The scientific interviews were extremely boring but after Ryan had kept Nemesis on his lap in the boat I did try and do a few. He was in the middle of explaining something brain-shrivellingly boring called electromagnetic resonance imaging when he suddenly stopped.

"Em," said Ryan to Shaggy, "do you remember a bit you filmed with . . . er . . . a strange dog attacking The Ag . . . I mean Dr Barns?"

Shaggy and Bobble looked at each other and mentally chewed this over for a while.

"Yerummm," Shaggy clicked his fingers floppily, "fête thing withmmm cheese-type stuff."

"Only," said Ryan, "she said she was going to use it to get the dog put down."

Shaggy turned the corners of his mouth down as if contemplating this, and Bobble went, "Um," and pointed at himself.

Shaggy said, "Ohermm, right."

Me, Boy Dave and Ryan leaned forward enquiringly.

"He, um," Shaggy jerked his head at Bobble, "s'already done it."

Bobble shrugged and opened the laptop. A few moments later we were looking at a film where Nemesis jumped up at The Agnetha's legs then (and it was really clever the way they did this) slid straight back down again and started licking herself.

"Wow," I stared at him, "that's brilliant. It looks just like she's being friendly."

"But how come?" asked Boy Dave. "We never said anything."

Shaggy snuffled. "He's against all, erm, cruelty to animals."

"Haven'term eaten meat for twenty years," said Bobble proudly.

"But you're just about to have a burger," I reminded him.

"*Vege*burger!" said Bobble indignantly.

*

By the time we got to Brighton the sun was going down. We sat at the edge of the marina looking out over the boats and all had double cheeseburgers with fries and banana milkshakes. Even Jefferson. The Crazy Frog Man skipped happily along the boardwalk with Confucius going, "Here, Champ. That's it. Good boy, Champ!" And feeding her bits of his cheeseburger. I think she liked being called Champ, and didn't seem to mind that Crazy Frog Man thought she was a boy.

After a bit he came over and pointed his finger at us. "Bad lads with big hearts!" He put on a television sort of voice, *"We tried touchy-feely. We tried discipline and tough love. Their last chance was a little brown dog called Rosy."* He looked as if he expected a round of applause.

"Nemesis," I said, "they're Confucius and Nemesis."

"Sounds like gardening," said the Crazy Frog Man confusingly. "We'll call her Rosy."

After that we just sat quietly while huge seagulls swirled over our heads, waiting for crumbs. Behind the millions of boat masts across the marina, the day was turning into night like blue ink leaking into ice cream.

All this time Jefferson had been standing on his own, eating his chips and looking out to sea over the rail. After a while I got up and went nervously over.

"Sir. . ."

He turned and looked sternly at me. Close up his face has little dips in it, as if one day he lay down on some gravel and the marks stayed for ever.

"I, er," I cleared my throat, "thank you very much, sir – about Nemesis."

Jefferson looked back at the boats. "No time for the 'uman race, boy. Bunch of scum, that's what we is. Dogs, see, know the meaning of loyalty." For a minute he looked thoughtful, then he said, "The name of that dog, Nemesis, that's a tank, that is. There was a tank out in Kuwait called Nemesis."

"That's pretty cool," I told him.

In the van on the way back we called our mums. Mine said, "Jordan, tell me the things I'm hearing aren't true." (And she said this in a really scary way, actually.)

Ryan's mum asked if he'd had a chance to do many watercolours because the light was so nice at this time of year.

Boy Dave's mum said, "David, I think you should know that as far as your dad's concerned you're toast."

Fifty

Mostly this story has a happy ending, but there was a weird bit to do with The Agnetha.

I had to go into a room with lots of kiddy toys and dolls and stuff. The Agnetha was waiting in there already. She looked quite normal again and her hair was flat-ish.

"Jordan!" she said as if she was really pleased to see me. "How are you? Take a seat."

The only place to sit was on a beanbag, so I stayed standing.

"I'm afraid I've got a lot to do today," I told her, "so if we just get on with it quite quickly."

"Well," she squidged herself down on to another beanbag, "I'm going to take the weight off my feet for a while."

After that she asked a whole load of questions about the woods and the air raid shelter. She kept saying, "Was there anyone else with you? Were there any grown-ups there?"

"To be honest with you," I told her, "I'm as surprised as you are. There we were, collecting twigs and sticks, and the next minute there were sheep everywhere and you had gone into the air raid shelter."

She coughed. "I think you and I both know there's a little more to it than that. You know you can talk to me about anything you want?"

This went on for far too long. It was like being a criminal on *The Bill* or something. In the end I said what they always say:

"Well, you and I both know there isn't a jury in the land who will convict on that sort of evidence, so you might as well let me go."

"Ah-ha!" said The Agnetha, "now we're getting somewhere. Who told you to say this?"

I sighed. "OK, I'll tell you everything but on one condition."

"Name it," she said.

"You let the others go."

"Oh-kay," she said slowly, "I'll see what I can do."

I sat down. "Look, it all started with the spaceship on the science-lab roof. . ."

I explained about the strange ringing in our ears and about how the aliens had been telling us what to do ever since, and about how that night we'd heard the sound of devouring and something heavy being dragged and piteous screams of "please spare me". Then I explained how the aliens came down in a blaze of green light and made us eat the offal, which was called "the tempting things" and how they made us gather up a few sticks. Then the next thing we knew, there were aliens everywhere disguised as sheep and that was when we ran away.

Boy Dave went in next and told her something about a bloke who looked a bit like Santa Claus who had a big sack and a sleigh with six huge rats. He was singing a weird song to himself as he sprinkled things from his sack into the air raid shelter, which went: *'A sprinkling, a sprinkling, a sprinkling I must go.'*

We went and tried to stop him but the largest rat called Mustaveadonut started to eat the second largest rat called Mustaveajammydodger, and all that was left was his tail hanging out of his mouth, so we just started to gather a few sticks when, for some reason, there were sheep everywhere and we got scared and ran away.

Ryan said a *whole* lot of stuff and I'm not totally sure if it had anything to do with what happened. If Daisy had been there she could have calmed him down but she wasn't and I think his interview with The Agnetha lasted most of the day. Also he decided to dress up as a medieval person in a pair of Daisy's tights, which I shouldn't think helped much.

When our mums and dads got a letter from The Agnetha, Dad wrote back. It took him ages because he's about as slow at writing as he is at reading. This is what it said:

DEAR DR BARNS,

I WOULD HAVE THOUGHT THAT WITH YOU BEING A CHILD PSYCHOLOGIST YOU WOULD KNOW A WIND-UP WHEN YOU SAW ONE.

YOURS FAITHFULLY,

DOMINIC SMITH

Then, to save writing one himself, Big Dave signed it too.

Ryan's mum got a letter as well, which Ryan said was as long as book. She didn't bother to write back but she did use it in a sort of sculpture. Apparently there's a famous woman who gets things from her past and makes an exhibition out of them – like she got her old bed and the cigarette packet her uncle was holding when he died and made a sculpture out of them. Ryan's mum was doing the same sort of thing, so the letter from the The Agnetha got stuck on to their old settee, along with an old dog's bone and a pair of false teeth, which had belonged to her grandfather.

The Agnetha did try to get some of her reputation back by doing an interview with the local paper about young village people being involved in evil rituals.

The headline said, **FAMOUS PSYCHOLOGIST SUFFERS FROM STRESS BECAUSE OF INCIDENT IN LOCAL WOOD**. (They could have put, **MEGA PYSCHO DRIVEN CRAZY IN BLOOD AND GUTS DRAMA**, but there you go.) Anyway, most likely they were scared of people finding out about the real goings on of the Women's Institute and the village hall committee's annual human sacrifice, because The Agnetha story was way smaller than the one called **LOCAL MAN GROWS PINEAPPLE**.

Fifty-one

When the time came for Nemesis to leave hospital Joanna and me set off with a basket. We don't really like having to talk to each other, but Joanna was actually trying to be a bit nice because she was really happy about Nemesis. Luckily we hadn't gone too far when there was the sound of an engine coming up the road behind us. It was my dad in the small works truck that they normally use to carry the cement mixer.

"On the way to pick up the rat?" he asked cheerfully as he pulled over.

We nodded.

"Hop in, then." He jerked his head to the back of the truck.

It was like I was really young again and Joanna was still young, too, and not as stupid as she really is. It reminded me of all the times we'd gone on the back of the truck when we were kids and thought it was really exciting and hoped we could see people we knew just to wave at them. Joanna didn't even seem to mind all the bits of dried cement everywhere.

Nemesis looked great. Her fur was glossy and clean and her snobby little face looked snobbier than ever and her tail was massive and fluffy. When she saw us she wiggled, trying to get away from the nurse. Joanna took her and cuddled her and started to cry and Nemesis went, "MMMM MMMM MMMM," really loudly and happily.

She rode home on the back of the truck with us and really enjoyed poking her head over the edge, watching the world go by.

Mum and Dulcie were waiting back at the house with her present: a massive cushion with a pattern like a tiger. They'd laid it out carefully beside the gas fire in the living room.

If this was a proper story I would be telling you now that Nemesis went over and looked at it wonderingly as if to say "Is this really for me?". She would gaze back over her shoulder with happy tears in her eyes before nervously stepping on to it and curling up cosily. Obviously none of this happened and she looked at the tiger cushion in disgust and jumped on to dad's chair and went to sleep.

Dad folded his arms and frowned.

"Dad," I said, "I think the best thing is if you sit on the tiger cushion for a bit, just until you've ... er ... made a dent in it, then she might start to like it."

Dulcie said, "I think the best thing might be to put

229

the cushion over Dominic's chair so that she has to get used to lying on it."

Dad said, "And I'm supposed to sit where exactly?"

"You can sit on another chair," Mum told him. "There's no law says you always have to sit in that chair, is there?"

Joanna said, "Like, if we put something of Dad's on her cushion? So it smelled the same?"

And this went on for a while until Dad said crossly, "I don't believe I'm even having this conversation." And stomped off back to work. At the front door he shouted back crossly, "I want that dog off my chair when I get back from work, you hear me? OFF my chair," and slammed the door.

Actually, the next time Dad got to sit on his chair was when all Boy Dave's family came round to watch the documentary. I think even Dulcie agreed that it was too humiliating for Dad to admit to Big Dave that he had to let a dog have his chair all the time.

I won't bother to tell you much about it, except to say that it was all pretty embarrassing, and everyone, except for me and Boy Dave, laughed massively and our mums cried at the bit where we rescued "Rosy".

They'd all brought drinks and food round and were treating it as some kind of a party, and Joanna was a total cringe around Boy Dave's brother, Craig, and had a huge strop because she wasn't allowed any wine.

The Agnetha in the air raid shelter was funny, though; they managed to make it seem like she was in there for hours.

I should probably say that, in the end, Mrs White and Dulcie became great friends. Dulcie kept saying, "Oh, by the way, I'm expecting Betty White for tea this afternoon." And they would insist on going in the front room and having tea in a teapot and proper cups, and the dogs did quite a lot of damage in there, actually.

Still, Dad was in a good mood because he and Big Dave had been given the contract to build the new school gym. We tried to make them put in a secret escape hatch but they said, "Cage, more like," and thought this was really hilarious.

Lastly, we did go to London. It was the whole of our class in the end and Miss Fairjoy and Jefferson were in charge of us. I should say at this point that Jefferson, who seemed to have gone badly back to how he usually is, was totally weird around Miss Fairjoy. He kept trying to hold the door open for her and was the colour of those sweets called "shrimps" for the whole time.

We did actually go through the door of Madame Tussaud's and wandered around a bit going, "Ooh, it's amazing – just like a real person" (again). But after a bit we sneaked back down and headed through the door.

"Where shall we go?" I asked as we trawled along the edge of the canal.

Ryan consulted a bit of paper, which he was calling an "itinerary".

"OK, I thought we'd head down here to Camden Market. From there we get the tube to Soho and visit Chinatown. Then there's a rather interesting building I'd like to see and, of course, the Science Museum. . ."

"No," said Boy Dave firmly. "No buildings or boring stuff."

That evening we were having a barbecue in the woods. Claire and Daisy were coming and we were going to cook sausages. Today was going to be brilliant.

**Read all about Jordan, Boy Dave
and Ryan's other adventures!**

When the new kid sucked Boy Dave
into a crazy computer-obsessed world and
made him a gaming zombie, we knew we had
to do something. Me and Ryan just wanted to
remind him the real world was fun.

We didn't know everything around
us would get annihilated. . .

WARNING! VAMPIRES are LiVing next Door!

Author shortlisted for the Roald Dahl Funny Prize

Dinah Capparucci

When vampires moved in next door and my vile uncle came to stay, we had to act before I was devoured or went insane! It would've been easier to fight the evil if me, Boy Dave and Ryan hadn't been grounded for life.

We didn't know our battle for survival would end in catastrophe. . .